# THE MEDICO ON THE TRAIL

# THE MEDICO ON THE TRAIL

JAMES L. RUBEL

CUTTING EDGE

The characters and events portrayed in this book are fictitious. Any similarity to real persons, living or dead, is coincidental and not intended by the author.


ISBN-13: 978-1-957868-97-4

Published by
Cutting Edge Books
PO Box 8212
Calabasas, CA 91372
www.cuttingedgebooks.com

# CHAPTER ONE

IT WAS high noon in the little town of Painted Springs. A hot, brassy sun blazed down to dry the dust of the street into a fine powder that the wind lifted and whirled around the heads of the two saddled ponies that stood hitched to the rail in front of the medico's office.

Except for these two horses, the town was completely deserted. The Lone Deuce, Painted Springs' only saloon, whose owner boasted that it never closed from sunup to sunup, had its swinging bat-wing doors backed by solid oak ones, and the brass padlock shone in the sun.

The Mansion House, the biggest of the town's false-fronted buildings, like the saloon facing it, was deserted. The only difference was that Maw Blane, who ramrodded it, had not taken the trouble to close its doors. Instead she had hung a sign on one of the windows which read, "Gone to a wedding. Will open for supper as usual."

The Rogers Mercantile Store, Painted Springs' house of bargains, and a place where you could buy anything from canned goods to Colt cartridges, had its shades drawn tight, and, like at the Lone Deuce, a heavy padlock hung from the lock on its door.

The doors of the livery stable stood wide open, but there was no hostler whittling in front of it, no one to feed and unsaddle the mount of any passing traveler. Like Tim Roney and Maw Blane, like Henry Rogers, "Shorty" Weaver had gone to a wedding.

In fact, the whole town had gone to a wedding. This was the day on which Nancy Starweather, orphaned owner of the S Bar 8 sheep ranch, had promised to take Doctor Cliff Monroe for better or for worse. Even the lowliest peon, the poorest Mexican sheepherder had been invited.

The two ponies at the hitching rail seemed tired of waiting. One of them was a big raw-boned gelding with a white blaze on his face. The other was a steel-dust stallion, clean of limb and with the build of a thoroughbred. On his back was a brand new black saddle, silver-studded, and with a silver-trimmed bridle to match.

Dorr Plum came out of the sheriff's office and stood for a moment tightening his string tie while his glance swept the town's main thoroughfare. A long black frock coat hung from his wide but bony shoulders; the stag butts of a pair of long-barreled Colts protruded from the tails of the clerical garment; and a wide-brimmed black felt hat, only recently brushed and cleaned, sat at a rakish angle on his grizzled head.

He took a heavy gold timepiece from his waistcoat pocket, glanced at it, and then, with a sudden squaring of his shoulders, marched down the planked walk to the medico's office and started up the rickety stairs.

Doctor Cliff Monroe was standing in front of a cracked mirror, trying to make a presentable knot in his tie. "Why," he demanded testily of the sheriff, as Plum's stocky figure showed in the doorway, "does a man have to look like a fashion plate to get married? Damn this cussed tie!"

The sheriff's wide face crescented into a grin that made his faded eyes twinkle merrily. "You look like a sheep bein' led to the slaughter," he chided. "I never have seen a groom yet that wasn't plumb scared to death. Buck up, son! I reckon it ain't goin' to be as bad as some folks make out. It's what comes after that's hard to take. Wait till that filly starts ridin' herd on you. There ain't no prettier gal in the state, but she's got a temper and a will of her own, and you're a-goin' to have to keep a tight rein on her."

Cliff Monroe was taller than the lawman, twenty years his junior, but with the same breadth of shoulders. Wide-spaced grey eyes looked out frankly on the world from a face that was tanned to the color of roasted coffee. He was dressed in conventional garb, a single-breasted coat with four buttons, and his riding boots were hidden beneath the cuffs of his long trousers.

"I'm not scared, Dorr," he said with an easy grin, "but I don't mind admitting that I'll be glad when it's over. Have you got the ring?"

The lawman's face fell, and his eyes widened in sudden fear. "God Awmighty!" he exclaimed. "I reckon I clean forgot it." He turned and made a sudden dive down the stairs, his high-heeled boots sounding hollowly as he headed for his office.

"If your head wasn't tied on," Cliff yelled after him, "you'd forget that. You're a fine best man. Next time I'll hire me a professional."

But the lawman was back in just a few moments, grinning again. "Had the pesky thing in my pocket all the time," he laughed. "And I heard that partin' shot you made. You don't know it yet, but things is goin' to be reversed pronto."

The medico quit working on his tie and turned his glance toward his friend. "Do you mean you and Maw?" he asked. "Why, Dorr, you coyoting old buzzard! I didn't think you had the nerve to ask her."

"I ain't yet," the lawman replied sheepishly, "but I'm a-goin' to. Got to have somebody to look after my rabbits and cook my vittles. Honest to Pete, Cliff, the pesky little critters is gettin' me. You know I only started with six pair three months ago, and already the warrens is full of young 'uns. Criminy! At the rate them critters has babies, the whole county's goin' to be overrun with 'em. I'll have to buy out your sheep ranch to hold 'em."

"Sounds better than the cow business to me," the medico remarked.

"You're danged tootin' it is. Them critters multiply in arithmetical progression. I read that in one of the government folders. You take one pair of rabbits, and if you leave 'em alone, and none of 'em die or gets killed, in three years you'll have thirteen million of 'em. Figure that out. And the hides is worth twenty cents apiece."

"Sounds like the man that used to sell that eye remedy," Cliff chuckled. "There's fifty million people in these United States, and every one of them has two eyes. Gentlemen, there's millions in it!"

"Go ahead and cackle," the lawman answered, just a little peeved. "But it's me that'll have the last laugh." Once again he pulled the big gold watch from his pocket and squinted at it. "You'd better get a move on, Cliff. We've only got an hour to the weddin'. And you'd better not keep the bride waitin'. It's bad luck. I'm a-goin' to get you there on time or bust a leg tryin'."

The sound of hoofs came from the street, startling both men. The town had been as quiet as a tomb now for at least three hours.

"Who in tarnation do you reckon that is?" the lawman demanded.

"You might go and see," Cliff suggested. "I'm ready now. I'll be right down."

The sheriff clumped down the steps and, a moment later, the medico followed. The sight that met his eyes was far from reassuring. Plum was helping a puncher to lift himself from the saddle. It was "Whitey" Snow, one of Jim Croll's S 4 boys. The man's face under his grease-stained Stetson was pain-twisted and white. When the sheriff got him to the ground, Cliff saw that one leg hung broken and useless. If Plum hadn't grabbed him and if Cliff hadn't leaped to help, the puncher would have collapsed.

"What in tarnation we a-goin' to do now?" the lawman grumbled.

"Fix him up, of course," Cliff gritted. "We'll put him in my office, Dorr. I can set the bone in a hurry, if it's nothing more than a broken leg."

"But the weddin', Cliff," the lawman protested. "You'll be late for it. That's bad luck."

"Then I'll have to be late," Cliff answered sharply. "I can't leave Whitey here with a broken leg."

Still grumbling, the sheriff helped Cliff carry the man up the stairs and into the office, where he walked back and forth like a caged lion, while Cliff removed the puncher's levis and boots and exposed the injured limb. Plum kept his big watch in his hand, and his glance kept leaping to it.

The hour for the wedding arrived, and Cliff was still working over the puncher.

"Dang it all, Cliff," the lawman exploded finally, "Nancy 'll be havin' conniption fits."

"Dorr," Cliff said sharply, turning to the lawman, "I can't leave things like this. You take the steel-dust and hightail it out to the ranch. Tell Nancy what has happened. I'll follow just as soon as I can. She'll understand."

"I reckon I better," the sheriff said, with a shrug and a deep frown. "But you get there just as quick as you can."

Plum didn't wait any longer. He went down the stairs, unhitched the steel-dust, swung himself to its back and headed across the manzanita-speckled flats for the Starweather ranch.

The big sheep ranch was in festive regalia when he arrived. Beneath the drooping cottonwoods that lined the banks of the dry stream, long wooden tables had been set up. Smoke spiraled upward in the breathless air from the hot beds of the barbecue pits, carrying the pungent odor of cooking meats. Two Mexican sheepherders were busy with long forked sticks, turning the sizzling meat.

Scattered among the trees, and lounging by the charred remnants of the big barn that had burned down several months previously, were groups of cowhands and groups of sheepmen. The punchers and cowmen wore freshly polished boots, clean Levis, and gaudy-colored shirts. Every man had a cartridge-studded gun belt about his waist, but for this occasion they had left their weapons with Poke Bonnett, the new sheriff-elect of the county.

But the sheepmen had neither the flare for dress nor the good looks of the cowmen. They wore loose cotton shirts and jeans stuffed into flat-heeled, high boots. They were a weather-beaten, gaunt-framed lot of men, with unkempt hair only partly combed, not slicked down and greased like the punchers'.

The women stood in groups about the wide veranda of the ranch house, their voluminous calico skirts out-flung, their breasts and waists tightly laced into bodices. They were far from comfortable-looking. The sun was hot, and the hours of waiting for the wedding had dampened their spirits.

The sheriff brought his mount to a halt in front of them, turned the reins of the two ponies over to a Mexican boy who came running, and, with a long face, passed the women by and entered the house.

Nancy Starweather sat just inside, her skirts billowing out from the leather armchair in which she reclined. She got up quickly when she saw the lawman and came towards him. Even in the semi-darkness of the big living room, her bright hair shone like spun gold.

"Where's Cliff?" she asked, worry filling her gentian-blue eyes.

Dorr told her what had happened. "I reckon there ain't anythin' to do but wait, Nancy. Cliff couldn't very well leave Whitey there with a busted leg. And he said he'd hurry. Shouldn't take him more than an hour."

Claire Napier, Nancy's school chum from El Paso, came from the window where she had been standing and put a hand on her friend's arm.

"You'll have to expect things like this, Nancy," she warned, "when you're married to a doctor." Unlike the owner of the sheep ranch, Claire Napier was dark of hair and eyes, with a trim figure, tightly laced so as to show every womanly curve. More than one cowhand in the section had looked on her with desire.

Twin spots of color burned in Nancy's cheeks and her eyes flashed with anger. "You'd think," she said, a little bitterly, "that he would at least be here in time for his wedding."

"But it couldn't be helped, Nancy," the lawman protested, standing up for his friend. "Whitey was mighty bad hurt. And it won't be long. Cliff 'll hurry as fast as he can. Lord knows, he's waited long enough for this."

Nancy did not say anything. She turned her back and, biting her lips to hold back the anger that welled up, moved over and sat down in the chair again, eyes straight ahead, her mouth a grim line.

The sheriff turned and went out. "Had a mite of a delay, folks," he announced, and his big voice boomed across the wide yard, reaching all the way to the barbecue pits. "Whitey Snow busted a leg, and the doc had to set it 'fore he'd come. Make yourselves to home." He stepped down into the yard and started walking towards the keg that was bolstered up on a couple of saw horses beneath one of the cottonwoods.

"Come on, gents," he cried. "This may be a mite out of order, but the sun is hot and I'm honin' to wet my whistle. Gather around, you mavericks and woolly nurses. Here's to the prettiest bride and the finest medico that this county's ever seen."

William Bonnett, known to his friends as Poke, and the newly elected sheriff of the county, joined Plum at the keg, followed by the cowmen. The sheepmen hung back, feeling a little out of place in this gathering consisting preponderantly of cowhands.

Poke Bonnett was a big man, six-foot-three of bone and muscle, with hands as big as hams and a homely face that wore a perpetual grin. A single bone-handled Colt swung at his thigh. Now he added his voice to the sheriff's, calling on the men to gather around the keg, and singling out several of the sheepmen.

"Come on, Clem, Sam! This is a weddin', not a burial. Liquor up, gents. The drinks is free."

But the sheepmen still hung back, and Plum, taking Bonnett aside, said, "The durned woolly nurses. They're still carryin' a chip on their shoulders. I recollect somethin' in the Bible like this, when it said the sheep 'ud lay down with the lion. Look at Sam Mullaby and Clem Jeffries. They both look like they was attendin' a wake instead of a weddin'." Again the sheriff pulled out his watch, and a deeper frown creased his brows. "I always get worried when this county has a shindig like this. It's like settin' on a powder keg. You can't mix cowmen and sheepmen together."

Bonnett chuckled deeply and put his big hand on the sheriff's shoulder. "You old moss horn," he chided. "Never did I see a man with such a nose for trouble. You ain't got nothin' to worry about. Another week and you're finished with the sheriffin' job. Besides, you ain't neither flesh nor fowl. You're a rabbit rancher."

This brought a laugh from the cowmen grouped about the keg, and the lawman had to take a lot of good-natured banter over his new profession.

"All right," he exploded. "You can all laugh, but I don't need no herders nor waddies clutterin' up my spread and eatin' me out of house and home. I'll be drivin' a spankin' team of thoroughbreds when the rest of you are headin' for the poorhouse. One pair of rabbits 'll raise thirteen million in three years. That's more than you can say for a thousand cows."

"You callate there'll be any room left for us in this county, Dorr?" Jim Croll badgered. The S 4 rancher was a tall, big-chested, grizzled man, with drooping cowhorn mustaches.

The sheriff did not get a chance to answer, for someone yelled to him from the house, and he turned and walked that way. A rider was cutting across the flats, a lone rider. At first the lawman thought it was his friend, arriving at last for his wedding, for it was his own sorrel pony, but Dorr's heart sank when he saw that on the back of the horse was not the doctor, but a ragged kid of nine or ten. It was young Otto Jungward, the son of a nestor who had just taken a piece of land close to the Springs to homestead.

The boy brought the big roan to a halt in front of the group of women, saw the sheriff, and addressed him. "The medico told me to tell you that you'd have to call the weddin' off, Sheriff. He ain't comin'."

A sudden hush fell over the women on the veranda; the boy was the focal point for all their surprised glances.

Dorr walked over to the horse and stood there, looking up at the younker. "Why ain't he comin'?" he demanded. "Can't he leave Whitey?"

"Tain't Whitey," the boy answered, just a little sullenly. "It's my sister. She's mighty sick. Dad brought him out there to see her. Doc says she's got pneumony. He can't leave her—not even for a weddin'. He said Miss Starweather 'ud understand."

Nancy, who had heard the announcement, came out on the porch. Anger had drawn all the color from her face, leaving it as white as the wedding dress she wore. Her blue eyes were like twin bonfires, blazing with wrath.

"You can go back and tell the doctor," she rapped out, "that I do understand—perfectly. There will be no wedding, not today, tomorrow nor ever." Grim-lipped, she turned on her heels and vanished into the house's dark interior.

"God Awmighty!" the lawman ejaculated. "God Awmighty! Now ain't that a pretty kettle of fish!"

# CHAPTER TWO

CLIFF had just finished setting the puncher's leg, and was wondering what he was going to do with him, when he glanced at his watch. It was already past three o'clock. He was now an hour late for the wedding, and he didn't see how he could leave Whitey here with no one to watch him. The man couldn't walk, and the town was completely devoid of help in any shape or form.

Whitey Snow, flat on his back, with his leg lying straight in front of him and lashed to splints, sensed the medico's dilemma. "You should have left me till after the weddin', Doc," he said, with a pain-twisted grimace. "I'm sure sorry I barged in on you like this. I clean forgot about it bein' your day to get spliced. I was a mite scared when that bronc kicked me, what with all the S 4 boys gone to the shindig and nobody to help me."

"Nonsense, Whitey." Cliff went to the basin and washed his hands. "You've only got two legs, and they're worth taking care of. What's worrying me now is what I'm going to do with you. I don't like to leave you here alone."

"Don't let that fret you," the puncher replied, trying to smile. "I'll get along. I left word at the ranch about what had happened. One of the boys 'll come and get me soon as they come home. You run along to your weddin'. And I'm wishin' you lots of luck."

"Sure you'll be all right?" Cliff asked.

"Course I will, Doc. But you'd better quit augerin' and hightail it. They say it's bad luck to be late to your weddin'."

Cliff didn't waste any more time. He put on his coat, took a last look at his tie, and raced down the stairs. It took him only a minute to reach the stable and find the sheriff's sorrel pony, already saddled and waiting. He lifted himself to the saddle and, ducking his head to avoid cracking it on the barn door, kneed the pony out into the street.

He had just reined it towards the south when a shrill yell made him bring the pony to a halt, and he turned in his saddle to see who was calling him. A single rider was coming down the street at a full gallop, his arms flapping with each beat of his mount's hoofs, his seat leaving the saddle with each heave of the animal's broad flanks.

"Doc! Doc!" the rider yelled as he came closer.

Cliff cursed under his breath at this new interruption, but he held the sorrel in and waited till the man had reined in, facing him. It was Jan Jungward, the big, bearded nestor who had homesteaded a piece close to the Springs.

"It's Shan!" the nestor gasped. "My daughter, Doc!" He was breathing heavily; excitement had definitely taken hold of him and was riding him with a tight rein. "She's terrible sick, Doc."

"This is my wedding day, Mr. Jungward," Cliff rapped out, anger tightening the lines about his mouth. Like the rest of the people of the community, Monroe did not have much use for the new settler, a sullen, bull-headed man who acted as if the world owed him a living.

Jungward's hairy hands gripped the horn of the worn saddle, and his big mouth twisted with fear and pleading. "You've got to come, Doc," he gritted. "You've just got to. She's dyin', Doc. My little girl! My Shan! You wouldn't leave her to die, would you, Doc?"

"I'm an hour late, Mr. Jungward," Cliff snapped coldly. "Your daughter will have to wait until after the ceremony. I'm sure she isn't as bad as you imagine her to be." Cliff had seen the girl once in town, and remembered her as a tough-tongued young hellion, a hoyden, who rolled her eyes at the punchers and sheepmen, and brazenly flaunted her full-breasted figure and pretty face in front of them.

Jungward had a gun belt encircling his thick waist, and now his hand darted down to unsheath the heavy Colt and to level it at the medico. "Damn you," he gritted. "I don't care if there's six gals waitin' to marry you. You're comin' to see my daughter. She's terrible sick, I tell you. If you don't come, Doc, so help me, I'll blast you right out of that saddle."

It wasn't the threat of the gun that made Cliff change his mind—it was the man's grimness, and the medico's certainty that the girl was really sick. The hoeman would hardly resort to such tactics unless his daughter were really ill. And no man realized his own responsibilities better than the medico. In spite of the fact that the woman he loved was waiting to become his wife, his plain duty was with this nestor.

"Put your gun away, Jungward," he said quickly. "It isn't necessary. I'll come with you, but I'll have to get my kit." He swung off the sorrel and hurried back to his office.

"Cripes, Doc!" the injured puncher exclaimed, as the medico came hurrying in. "You're a-goin' to miss that weddin' entirely if you don't hurry."

"I'm afraid you're right, Whitey," Cliff answered grimly. "I *am* going to miss it. If anyone comes looking for me, tell them that I had a call to Jungward's spread. He has a sick daughter who needs immediate attention."

"Jungward!" the puncher exploded. "That sodbuster? Good gravy, Doc! Have you plumb lost your mind?"

Cliff didn't answer. He was already taking the rickety steps three at a time. The die was cast. By the time he had called on the nestor's daughter, even if she weren't so sick as her father thought she was, it would be too late to reach the Starweather spread in time for the ceremony.

A second later he and the homesteader were thundering out of town, the big plow horse under Jungward having difficulty in keeping up with the sheriff's wiry sorrel, which was used to a rider, and whose long legs rose and fell with rhythmic cadence.

The Springs reared their cathedral-like spires ahead of them as they topped the rise and dipped down towards the bubbling fountain of water that earned the place its name of Painted Springs.

In the background stood the jig-saw line of hills, the higher peaks of the range, and the hollows, with their reservoirs of color. The mesa itself, dry now, was covered with grey-green cholla, while beyond it, at the limits of the county, the saffron-hued desert began. Here were Apache Plumes, dry and desiccated, shriveled greasewood, parched mesquite, and the waving plumes of ocotillo.

They drew rein in front of a cabin built of logs and adobe. The crude lean-to made of sahuaro poles and an even cruder barn built of uprights and thatched with grass were the whole extent of Jungward's spread. Poverty stared back at the visitor from every angle. A dilapidated prairie schooner, its wheels bending drunkenly inward, stood gaunt and deserted by the barn.

A woman came to the door: a frail-looking creature in a ragged calico dress, a woman whose tired face showed the marks of past prettiness. Like her husband, fear had her in its grip, and she was twisting her blue-veined hands together. In back of her crowded a boy of ten, the living image of his father, short and husky, with a round face.

Cliff dropped from his horse and moved towards the woman, his kit in his hand. As she made room for him to enter, he put his hand on her arm reassuringly, moved by the fear he saw tightening her thin lips.

"I'm sure there is nothing to worry about, Mrs. Jungward," he said.

She did not answer; she just stood there watching him as he moved inside, her faded blue eyes round and terrified. And when, with quick strides, he had reached the patient's bedside, she was directly in back of him.

Cliff could smell the fever in the close confines of the little cabin, and his glance narrowed on the sick girl, who lay with her bright hair spread fan-wise over the grey pillow slip, perspiration beading her high white brow, froth that was crimson-flecked bubbling at her full lips. He was glad now that he had come. Shan Jungward was sick. Her father had not been wrong.

He set his kit on the floor and took the girl's limp wrist in his hand. The pulse was fast—too fast. He found his thermometer and pushed it gently between her lips. He had not realized how pretty a girl she was. The hair spreading across the pillow was as bright and coppery as a new penny. Her eyes were closed now, but he remembered that, when she had looked at him in town, they had seemed to be cataloguing what she saw and filing it away for future reference. They had been strange eyes, he recalled, tawny, shot with flecks of green.

When he withdrew the thermometer to read it, a sudden cough racked the girl's body, bringing more perspiration to her brow and dampening the cotton nightgown about her throat.

Straightening, he asked the nestor's wife how long she had been sick.

"About four days," the woman answered, fear again widening her eyes.

Four days! Cliff knew the symptoms. The crisis could not be far off. It was pneumonia in the advanced stages. And she could not be left here in this draughty cabin if they hoped to save her.

"I want a jacket made, Mrs. Jungward," he snapped at the nestor's wife. "A short jacket of wool or flannel. Use one of the blankets if necessary. There is no time to lose. She's worse than I thought she was. It's pneumonia. And she can't be left here. We'll have to move her into town."

A sudden scream burst from the girl's lips, followed by a torrent of words that made Cliff look at her with new appraisal. Her eyes were wide open and staring. Her mother started toward her, but Cliff held her back.

"She's delirious," he said. "I'll watch her. You start work on that jacket." He moved back to the patient's side and took the girl's wrist in his strong fingers.

The pressure of his hand seemed to calm her. Her talk subsided, and her glance focused finally on the medico's face. And then, suddenly, a smile crescented her lips. "Hello, Doc," she said huskily. "How come you're here? I thought you were gettin' married today."

"Not today, Miss Jungward," Cliff answered, shaking his head. "No wedding until we see you through. I'm going to take you into town with me. Maw Blane's going to nurse you and look after you."

"Gee, Doc," she breathed, "that'll be swell." The words brought on another fit of coughing, and red froth again crimsoned her lips.

Jan Jungward came across the room and put his hand timidly on the medico's arm. "I don't know how to thank you," he muttered, "but maybe God'll square things for the trouble we've caused. Shan's my little girl, no matter what folks say about her.

If anything happened to her, I reckon it'd just about kill Mother and me. You think she'll be all right?"

Cliff nodded his head reassuringly, and then, trying to arouse these two out of the fear that gripped them, snapped, "Go hitch up your team and bring it around in front. And can that boy of yours ride?"

"Course he can," the man snorted. "Otto can ride anything on four legs."

"Good! Have him take the sorrel and ride to the S Bar 8. Tell him to find the sheriff and Miss Starweather and explain to them why I can't be there."

"You think they'll understand, Doc?" the man asked anxiously. "Folks hereabouts don't cotton to us hoemen. 'Specially the women. There are some who think my daughter ain't—"

"I don't care what anyone thinks," Cliff snapped impatiently. "Your daughter is desperately ill, Jungward, and the only chance I have to save her is to take her into town where she can get the proper care. Now hurry, man! Don't stand there arguing with me."

A moment later Cliff heard the youngster pound away across the mesa on the lawman's horse.

Mrs. Jungward's fingers were flying as she fashioned a jacket out of an old blanket, and, in the meanwhile, Cliff did what he could to relieve the suffering of his patient, but the girl was delirious again and muttering words that did not make sense. Only one name beat into the medico's brains as she repeated it time and time again. Clem!

The homesteader brought the schooner around to the front. Mrs. Jungward had finished the jacket. Cliff lifted the girl's shoulders while the mother slipped it on, pinning it close about her breasts and neck. When she had finished, he picked the patient up in his arms and strode towards the door.

"You're mighty sweet, Doc," Shan whispered to him, as he laid her gently on the bottom of the vehicle and pillowed her head on the straw her father had thoughtfully placed there. "I'm not worth all this trouble."

"You're worth your weight in gold," he answered briskly.

"Do *you* really think so?" she asked, and her green-flecked, tawny eyes were riveted to his.

"If I don't, your father and mother do. Now stop talking. All set, Jungward," he called to the nestor, who had helped his wife to the front seat and was now climbing up beside her. "The sooner we get this young woman to bed, the better."

Twilight was beginning to darken the range as the vehicle rolled down the town's main street and came to a halt in front of the Mansion House. Cliff climbed out, again picked up the now sleeping girl in his arms and strode up the steps. But he stopped suddenly, wide-eyed. The hotel's front doors were closed and locked, and tacked to the front of them was a freshly painted sign that read, "Closed for one month."

His glance swiveled around to sweep the street. Lights burned in the Lone Deuce and the sheriff's office, but, except for the single pony hitched to the rail in front of the Mercantile Store, the street was deserted.

"I'll have to take her to my office, Jungward," he said to the nestor, who was standing beside him. "For some reason, the hotel is closed."

Without waiting for a reply, he strode down the walk and up the stairs, with the hoeman and his wife close at his heels. He had counted on Maw Blane to help him out, and now, with the hotel closed and the proprietress gone, he didn't know what to do.

He placed the girl on his own bed and, striking a match, lit the lamps. He looked over at the couch where Whitey had been left, and was glad to see it was empty. Someone from the S 4 had come for the puncher.

"You folks had better go on home," he said to the nestor and his wife. "I'll get one of the Mexican women to look after her. I can bunk there on the couch until the crisis is past."

The stairs creaked suddenly under a heavy weight. "Cliff—" the sheriff called. Then he was standing in the doorway, letting his glance search the room and its occupants. The outflung light touched his gaunt features, etching into bold relief a sternness that was unusual. His two hands were hooked into his gun belt.

"God Awmighty!" he exploded suddenly. "You had the nerve to bring her here?"

"And why not, Dorr?" Cliff snapped. "She'd have died if I'd left her out at the Springs."

The lawman stood there for a long time, puzzled and angry. At length he rapped out, "Danged if I can figger you, Cliff. You know what folks say about—her." He inclined his head toward the girl on the bed, whose eyes were still closed, whose face was crimson from the high fever.

"I hate to be the one to bring you the news, but Nancy's through—finished. She told me to tell you. When a man thinks more of a nestor's gal than he does of her, I callate she's right."

Cliff reached the lawman in three quick strides. "Good God, Dorr," he gritted, "what in the devil are you talking about?"

The lawman nodded his head. "It's the truth, Cliff, and I can't blame her. Jim Croll came here an hour ago and took Whitey out to the spread. He allowed as how he wouldn't let no sawbones like you set the leg of a polecat. You sure made a mess of things, Cliff," he went on tonelessly. "Clem Jeffries made Nancy an offer on the spread. She's snapped it up. She and Maw and Claire are plannin' to take the first stage from here in the mornin'."

Cliff stepped back, his glance still on the sheriff's face. This sudden hatred that had flamed against him was past understanding. He had done nothing more than his plain duty. If he had arrived at the wedding on time, as the Lord knows he had planned to do, it would have meant the death of this girl, and perhaps irreparable injury to Whitey Snow. What kind of folks were these people of the mesa?

And then suddenly, looking at the nestor's long face, he realized what he was up against. Jungward and his family were outcasts, pariahs to the ranchers of this section. They were no better than the coyotes and wolves that ranged the higher peaks. The fact that the medico had gone to their succor definitely branded him as one of them. These cattlemen, with their hidebound ideals, could not understand the creed of a physician.

And suddenly Cliff was glad that he had done what he had. His grey eyes hardened, and leveled on the man whom he had considered his best friend.

"Dorr," he said icily, "I've always counted you as the best friend I had here, but you're a lawman, and I realize you don't understand a physician's oath. I loved Nancy and hoped to marry her. I still do, but—if that is her decision, I will have to abide by it."

The sheriff's glance again swept to the patient, then to the fear-ridden faces of the nestor and his wife, back finally to the medico's. "I reckon you've made your bed," he said at last. "*Adios!*" And he turned on his heels and clumped down the stairs.

# CHAPTER THREE

CLIFF had plenty of time during that long night to think, for no one bothered him. Watching beside the bed of his patient, he heard the beat of hoofs coming to and going from town, heard men's voices raised. At times he even heard his own name mentioned, and knew that the people of this county were talking about him.

But he shut it all out, concentrating on the job in hand. Shan was quiet and delirious by turns. She would sleep a little, and then suddenly, without warning, break into a torrent of words that were almost completely unintelligible.

"You're a swell guy, Doc," she said lucidly, when the town had quieted down and the night was almost over. "Why don't you try to get some sleep? I'm sure I'll be all right."

"Too much on my mind, Shan," he answered, shaking his head.

"Did she give you the gate?"

The question, coming as it did, startled him. He had thought she was asleep when the sheriff had come in. Yet it was not uncommon for patients suffering from pneumonia to hear things, even in their slumber, for their sleep was not deep.

"She did, Shan," he answered.

She put her hand out and rested it on his arm. "Gosh, Doc," she whispered, "that's tough. I'm sorry. And it's my fault. I ain't worth all this trouble."

"And what makes you think so, Shan? I'd do as much for anyone. But I can't understand Nancy. That's what worries me."

"I reckon you don't savvy the womenfolks, Doc," she said with a smile. "They don't like me. They think I'm a mite too brazen. Maybe I am, but I ain't hankerin' to spend the rest of my life milkin' cows and bein' poor. I'm goin' to get some place, and the only way I know how to get it is through a man. Nancy knows my mind. She was jealous when she found out you were at my place. She was hurt, too—hurt to think that you'd miss the weddin' to look after a no-account like me. Don't you savvy?"

"Sorry, but I don't, Shan. I thought Nancy loved me. I've about arrived at the point where I don't think she does or ever did. Yet why should she have promised to marry me if she didn't? That's what doesn't make sense. I'm just a poor country doctor with more patients than money. Nancy's rich, according to anyone's standards."

A sudden fit of coughing racked Shan, and Cliff leaned over to try and make her more comfortable. He got some morphine out of his cabinet, dropped it into some water and gave it to her. Then he sat by the bed, holding her hand and stroking her forehead, until her eyes closed and her breathing was deep and even. The morphine, he knew, would give her the rest she needed.

He walked to the window and stood there a moment, looking down into the darkness of the street. It was as if he were alone. No lights showed in the town. Even Tim Roney's saloon was dark. Finally, with a sigh, he stretched himself on the couch, lying there quietly, trying to put all thoughts out of his head, until at last sleep came.

A sharp knocking on his door awoke him. The sun was already cutting broad banners of light across his office floor, and he got up and moved hurriedly across the room before the noise disturbed his sleeping patient.

Poke Bonnett stood there, his huge bulk almost blocking the entrance. "Mornin', Cliff," he said, and his deep voice boomed like a bell across the stillness of the room. But when Cliff motioned him to silence, he lowered his voice. "I just wanted to tell you there's considerable feelin' over what you've done, and I've heard talk of lynchin' you. But I want you to know that I savvy plenty, and you can count on me. That old mossyhorn Plum had ought to be hamstrung and quartered. Is there anythin' I can do?"

Cliff thought of his patient's needs first, and nodded. "Now that the hotel is closed, and I have no place to keep Shan, I need a woman's help. If you'd ride out and ask Mrs. Geosta, I'd appreciate it. If she won't come, then go out to the Springs and get Mrs. Jungward. And thanks, Poke. I knew I could count on you."

"Count on me!" Bonnett barked back. "You'd ought to know me better than to doubt it. How's the gal?"

"About the same, Poke. I can't tell until the crisis is passed. That may be in twenty-four hours or three days."

The sheriff-elect had more to say, but he held himself in check for the moment and took his leave. Cliff got himself cleaned up and took a closer look at his patient. She was still sleeping, and sleep, he felt, was better medicine than anything he could give her.

Not wanting to leave the girl, he busied himself in cleaning his office and checking the air to see that there were no draughts. An hour passed, and Bonnett's heavy step sounded on the stairs. After him came Rosa Geosta. She was a big-breasted, wide-hipped Mexican woman whom Cliff had befriended before, and was no stranger to the sick room. She went to work immediately making the patient comfortable, and Cliff felt that he was leaving Shan in capable hands.

He and Bonnett moved down the stairs and out into the bright light of a new day. The stage had been rolled from the livery, and the hostler was just bringing the teams out to hitch them. Cliff walked on down the awning-covered walk to the Chinaman's new restaurant. It was the only eating-place in town, now that the Mansion House was closed.

Bonnett described the events of the day before to him. "I didn't hear all of it," he finished, "but Nancy looked like she could 've bitten steel rails in half, she was so mad." He chuckled suddenly. "But what Maw said to Dorr was worth hearin'. She sure bawled that old mossyhorn out, blamin' him for the whole thing. And she called him a two-bit rabbit rancher. That got under his skin plenty."

Cliff wasn't interested in how the community looked upon him, but the big sheriff-elect told him anyhow. "Bunch of powder-eatin' fools," he grated. "Clem Jeffries allowed as how you'd ought to be lynched for standin' up a girl at the altar. And danged if them other hotheaded idiots didn't agree with him."

Cliff finished his breakfast and strode outside, rolling a quirley with deft fingers. He had thought some of riding out to the S Bar 8 to try and make amends, but what Bonnett had told him had made him change his mind. It was not his place to go begging on his knees for another chance. His pride was too great for that and, strangely enough, the blow that had fallen no longer rankled so much. He had been right and Nancy wrong.

A group of riders pounded into town and came to a halt in front of the sheriff's office. Heading them was Jim Croll, the tall, raw-boned owner of the S 4 and Whitey Snow's boss. He dropped from his pony and started for Plum's quarters, but changed his course when he saw Bonnett and the medico, and turned their way instead.

"Lookin' for you, Doc," he announced, and there was no friendliness in his glance. "The Association held a meeting last night. We've decided that we want your resignation as county health officer."

Cliff met the man's steady glare coldly, weighing carefully what he said. Before he could answer, Bonnett sang out:

"I figured you had more sense, Croll. What's eatin' you? What the medico does to a sheepman's daughter ain't none of your business. Looks to me like that's personal, between him and her."

"Keep out of this, Poke," Cliff snapped. The lawman's talk had given him time to consider and to map out his plans. The small wage that he received as county health officer would have meant a great deal to him, married. It meant less than nothing now that Nancy had turned him down. He could live without feeling the pinch of poverty on the fees he could collect from his patients. But he had no intention of moving out, and he said so.

"You can have my resignation, Jim," he said, "any time you want it, but I'm not leaving. I've built my practice up in this community, and I intend to stay here."

"You will like blazes!" the rancher growled. "You can stay if you like, but you'll get no patients. We're seein' to that."

"And just how will you do that?" Cliff demanded, anger tightening the lines about his mouth.

Croll laughed nastily. "After what happened yesterday, there ain't a sheepman nor a cowman that 'ud let you minister to his dog. Stay if you want to, Doc, but you'll starve to death."

"You've overlooked one thing, Jim," Cliff pointed out. "You men have been so wrapped up in your own work you've failed to read the signs. All this range is open to homesteading now. It will be only a few months until you cowmen and sheepmen will be fighting for your lives. The railroad has reached Bremen. Nestors will be pouring into this country in greater and greater numbers."

The big rancher's face was slowly getting whiter and whiter as his anger rose. Bonnett saw it and put a restraining hand on his arm, but the man threw if off with an angry shake of his head.

"I always figgered you as smart, Doc," he rasped, "but it seems like a pretty face has gone to your head. Nestors! Sod-busters!" he mocked. "You think you can make a livin' out of the likes of them? They ain't never goin' to get a foothold in Painted Springs. We're seein' to that, and, by God, we'll run you out of town along with them."

With a defiant snort, the rancher turned on his heels and tramped back to his pony. He said nothing to the other riders, but the group instantly wheeled their mounts and followed him out of town at a fast gait.

"Danged if I ever seen such an ornery bunch," Bonnett growled. "This county no sooner gets out of one trouble than the jug-headed fools is tryin' to get into another ruckus. All hell's goin' to be poppin' in this town soon, and me, I'm the new sheriff and I got to keep the peace. Damn nestors!"

"Don't damn the nestors," Cliff chided, "unless you damn the rest of them."

Whereupon Bonnett left him to go on some errand.

Cliff walked up the street to Plum's office and turned in there, standing with his back to the door jamb and watching his friend. The sheriff was trying to clean up all his paper work before he turned his office over to Poke Bonnett.

"What in tarnation do you want?" the lawman growled suddenly, as he looked up and saw the medico.

It was so unexpected that Cliff's eyes widened and his lips parted. It was so unlike the gruff sheriff. But as Plum's glance continued to rake him without any sign of friendliness, Cliff reddened and, without a word, turned on his heel and went out.

Then the rattle of wheels and the screech of protesting brake blocks brought his attention around to the other end of town. A buckboard was coming in, and, as it drew closer, Cliff saw three women close-packed on the jump seat, with trunks and baggage piled in back of them. Clem Jeffries was driving.

The buckboard rolled to a halt, and Cliff felt the eyes of the three women concentrating on him. Just a little unwillingly, he turned his glance their way. The hostler came hurrying from the stable to help with the baggage, and Plum tramped out of his office, stepping from the walk into the street to greet them.

Cliff wanted to follow in the sheriff's footsteps, but pride held him riveted, and unconsciously he wiped the look from his eyes, fearful that this woman who had turned him down would see it and gloat.

But one of them was not deceived by him; and she came through the dust of the street, lifting her wide skirts, until she stood facing him.

"Cliff," she said, softly, "I'm sorry. I tried my best to make Nancy understand."

He looked down into the piquant oval face of Claire Napier, with her dark eyes and hair, and smiled faintly. "Thanks, Claire," he said. "And it's been a real pleasure knowing you. I hope some day our paths will cross again."

A smile crescented her lips, and she held out her hand for him to take. Cliff took it in his own strong fingers and pressed it tightly.

*"Vaya con Dios,"* he said softly. "Godspeed." And then, suddenly, he drew her into his arms and kissed her swiftly.

As he released her, he heard Nancy stifle a little cry, but he did not look at her. He turned on his heels and marched swiftly to his office, climbing the stairs like a man in a dream, and wondering what on earth had prompted him to do that. If he had slapped Nancy's face, it couldn't have been a worse insult.

He was at the top step when he heard the thud of boots following him, and he looked down to see Dorr Plum barge to the foot of the stairway and stop. His seamed face was twisted with anger.

"You two-timin' polecat," the lawman gritted up at him. "Come down here and I'll beat the tar out of you."

Cliff laughed bitterly. "Not today, Sheriff," he replied. "Some other time I'll be glad to accommodate you. Give my regards to your friends and tell them that I wish them a pleasant trip." With another grim chuckle he stepped into his office, closing out for good the sight of the women on the street.

He was administering an emetic to his patient when he heard the stage driver's whip crack. He was still there by his patient's bedside when the rattle of wheels and the clank of chains told him that the woman he had loved was going out of his life forever.

He forced all thoughts of Nancy from his mind and concentrated on Shan. She was worse. The crisis was coming swiftly, much more swiftly than he had expected. Her fever had mounted, and already her night-clothes were wringing wet with perspiration. The delirium had passed, and so had most of the cough, but her eyes were partly glazed, and she could not recognize even the medico.

Rosa Geosta fluttered about the room, bringing dry cloths to wipe her patient's forehead. Cliff did not move except to administer some new drug that he thought might help. He kept his fingers on Shan's pulse, watching her with his steady glance.

The sun rose higher and began to dip. Cliff was not conscious of time. He did not know that riders were coming into town. He was totally unaware of anything that happened on the street.

Twilight darkened the range. A light flamed in the Lone Deuce, and Rosa, taking her cue from that, struck a match and lit the lamp in the office. It touched the medico's grim face, bringing out all the hardness of the lines about his mouth.

And then, suddenly, Cliff saw the change that took place in the girl. Her eyelids fluttered and opened and, for the first time since morning, her eyes focused on him and recognized him.

"Hello, Doc," she whispered, weakly. "Ain't you married yet?"

Cliff got his thermometer out and gently pushed it between her lips. "Don't talk," he warned. "That's the last one of those I've got till the stage comes in." A minute later he pulled it out, studied it and heaved a sigh of relief.

"The crisis is past," he announced, and stood up, feeling suddenly tired and hungry after his day's vigil. "She's out of it, Rosa. Heat up some of the broth. All we have to do now is build up her strength."

The Mexican woman breathed a prayer of thanksgiving and crossed herself. Cliff grinned down at Shan and said, "You're on the mend, young lady. I'm going to ride out and tell your mother and father just as soon as I get something to eat."

He put on his hat and descended the steps to the walk, turning toward the Chinaman's. "I'll be having stomach trouble myself," he muttered aloud, "if I have to eat at that Chink's very long." But he turned in there, nevertheless, and after a little came out, feeling better.

There were men on the walks, but none of them spoke to him as he marched by, heading for the stable. Even Shorty Weaver, the bowlegged little hostler, was sullen and uncommunicative. Cliff saddled his roan himself and, lifting his body to the pony's back, kneed him towards the Springs.

It was dark now, with a blackness like a solid wall, but as he topped the rise, and the turrets and jagged upthrusts of the

Springs reared against the skyline, he saw a ruddy glare that made him rowel the pony to a swifter gait.

It was Jungward's spread. Reaching it, Cliff's eyes hardened. There was nothing left of it—nothing but the still red embers of the burned cabin and the charred and blackened uprights of the barn. Then his glance saw a sprawled body just a little way from the cabin. With a muttered curse, he dropped to the ground and reached the man.

It was Jan Jungward, and he was dead. Cliff knew that the instant he rolled the body over. Sightless yellow eyes stared up at him. A crimson stain had dyed the front of the nestor's shirt.

Grim-lipped, the medico ran to his spooky pony and headed back for town. There could be no peace in Painted Springs, he reflected bitterly.

# CHAPTER FOUR

CLIFF pushed the big roan to the utmost, for he was worried about the disappearance of the homesteader's wife and son, as well as about the possible repercussions of the murder.

But it was well past midnight when he drew rein in front of the sheriff's dark office and realized the lawman was not there. A strong light still burned in the Lone Deuce, and Cliff turned his steps that way, hoping against hope that he would find Plum there.

He swung his shoulders against the bat-wing doors, blinking in the bright light. And he was not disappointed. The sheriff, Jim Croll, and Clem Jeffries were all three standing at the bar, with Tim Roney leaning his elbows on the counter and listening to them. Over at a corner table, four punchers were having a spiritless game of poker.

All of them looked Cliff's way. Clem Jeffries scowled at him. Jim Croll gave him a friendless nod, and Dorr Plum glanced at him as if he had never seen him before. The Lone Deuce proprietor was the only one who gave him a welcome.

"You're ridin' late, Doc," he said. "Have a nightcap?"

The buzz of talk that the medico had heard ceased abruptly, and Cliff felt the eyes of the four poker players narrowing on him as he crossed the room and reached the bar.

"This place is beginnin' to smell like polecats," Jim Croll remarked, with a curl on his lips. "I reckon I'll head for home."

"Me, too," the sheep rancher seconded, and then, looking at Cliff, he added, "It's sure funny how sweet a dead coyote can smell alongside of a medico."

The two started for the door, intending to edge past Cliff, but he stopped them with, "I didn't come here to associate with killers and firebugs, but I thought you men would like to know that what you've been waiting for is here."

The big S 4 rancher stopped and glared at Cliff. "What in tarnation you drivin' at?" he demanded, and the medico saw the sheriff lean forward with a sudden new interest.

"Jan Jungward was murdered tonight," Cliff said in a flat, hard voice. "Shot through the heart, and his home burned down over his head. His wife and boy are missing. Perhaps one of you men can tell me more about it."

A sudden silence blanketed the room. Jim Croll turned his head and looked at the lawman. The four men at the poker table laid down their cards, and their glances swiveled to the sheriff's face.

"When did this happen?" Plum demanded. "Who did it?"

"I'm the county health officer, not the sheriff," Cliff answered coldly. "I think that's your job. I was taking the news out to them that their daughter would live. That, of course, wouldn't interest any of you gentlemen, as you've plainly showed you think she's lower than the wolves that prowl the Dragoons. You might ask Jim Croll," he added, his grey eyes raking the S 4 rancher's long face.

"What in tarnation?" the lawman exploded wrathfully. "Jim and Clem been with me all evenin'. You can't come in here accusin' innocent folks."

"I haven't accused anyone yet, Sheriff," Cliff replied sourly. "I just thought that Croll might know something about it, since he threatened me. Good night! No drink tonight, Tim," he said, turning to the proprietor. "I still have a very sick girl on my hands."

The S 4 rancher's face had drained white; with a sudden oath, Croll gripped the medico's arm and swung him around savagely. "Maybe runnin' you out 'ud be too good for you," he gritted. "Maybe a bullet in your guts 'ud knock some sense into your head."

Cliff shook off the offending arm. "Any time you'd like to try it, Croll," he snapped, "you know where to find me. You can count on one thing. You won't find me shooting helpless homesteaders, nor kidnapping their women and children."

The S 4 rancher let out another oath, and his hand streaked for his gun. Only a quick move on the sheriff's part prevented him from making good his threat.

"Easy, Jim," Plum warned. "The Doc ain't armed."

"The devil take this cussed country!" Tim Roney rapped out in exasperation. "Are we goin' to have another plagued range war? Never did I see such a herd of bantam roosters livin' in one country. But Jim and Clem couldn't of had nothin' to do with it, Doc. They've both been here since supper. How long did you figger the old coot had been dead?"

The bartender's question seemed to ease the tension. The S 4 rancher took his hand away from his gun butt, and some of the color returned to his face, although his blue eyes still glittered with anger.

"Good riddance!" the sheep rancher growled. "That's the proper way to treat them sod-busters. Maybe killin' a few of 'em 'll scare the rest of 'em out."

"He had been dead for some time," Cliff answered evenly, "but the cabin was still blazing. Now, if you men will excuse me, I'll return to my quarters." He turned on his heel and marched out stiffly. Not for anything in the world would he have let these men see how their coldness and obvious dislike affected him. But the one whose attitude hurt the most was the lawman. In the past, Dorr Plum had been his staunchest supporter and ally. They had faced death together. Cliff would have given his life for the weathered old sheriff.

He unsaddled the pony, turned him loose in the livery corral and, with leaden feet, marched back to his office. Rosa was sound asleep on the couch, but Shan's eyes were open, and she smiled at him as he came through the door.

"Did you see Mom and Dad?" she asked in a weak voice.

Then something in his face made her cry out, and he knew that she would have to learn the truth tonight. He came over and sat down by the bed. "I've got bad news for you, Shan," he said softly. "Mighty bad news."

"I knew it." Her voice was barely a whisper. "Ever since you left, I've had a feeling that somethin' was wrong. Tell me, Doc. I've got to know."

Trying to soften the blow as much as possible, he told her what he had found. "I think your mother and brother are safe, Shan. I could find no trace of them. Perhaps the killers took them away, intending to frighten them off."

Her hands clenched, and a grim look hovered around her lips. "Dad's dead," she whispered. And then, suddenly, her eyes were on the medico's, probing into their grey depths. "You know who did it? You got any suspicions?"

He shook his head, and took her hand, holding it tight in his strong fingers. "Not the faintest idea, Shan," he answered softly. "I just came from the sheriff. I think you can depend on him to leave no stone unturned to find the murderers, and your mother and brother."

"Dorr Plum!" she mocked bitterly. "That old coot's too old for the sheriffin' job. How long you figure I'm goin' to have to lie here?"

Her intentions were plain to him. He could see by the look in her tawny eyes, by the way she clenched her teeth, that, once on her feet, revenge would motivate all her actions. Nothing short of sudden death would prevent her from carrying on.

"That's pretty hard to say, Shan," he evaded. "Pneumonia is a mighty tricky business. Offhand, I'd say at least a month."

"A month! You mean I got to lie here four weeks, twiddlin' my thumbs, while them wolves prowl the range? God in heaven, Doc! I won't do it. You can't keep me here that long."

"I don't want to keep you here any longer than is absolutely necessary, Shan," he said gently. "But to try anything else would be suicide. You're still a mighty sick girl. The fact that the crisis has passed and the fever has broken doesn't help matters. For at least the next two weeks, I'll have to watch you carefully. A relapse might prove fatal. And I don't want anything to happen to you, now that the worst is over. It's late, and this talking is tiring. You go to sleep now and rest. In the morning, we'll discuss it further."

The hum of conversation had awakened Rosa. Cliff ordered some more hot broth for his patient, found an extra blanket in his cupboard, and stretched himself on the floor of his office for the night. Before he went to sleep he heard the sound of hoofbeats in the street, and knew that Plum was on his way to the scene of the crime, but he did not hear him return. The next morning, he saw a notice announcing the inquest into Jan Jungward's death tacked to the bulletin board that hung on the front wall of the Mansion House.

The news of the killing had spread fast and, even at this early hour, riders were moving into town and the hitch rails were filling up. And there was more than one hoeman in the ranks. As Cliff stood in front of the café, rolling a quirley, a big wagon rumbled into town from the direction of the Springs, with two gaunt, bitter-faced settlers on the seat, each with a worn scatter-gun across his lap. They hitched their team to the rail in front of the Mercantile and joined the swelling crowd that had gathered there.

Cliff had never felt quite so ostracized. He knew only a few of the settlers by name, and these nodded to him in a friendly way, but the men with whom he had ridden, the men whose wives and children he had doctored neither spoke to him nor looked at him. The ranchers of the county had apparently pegged him into a hole of their own making. The man who would leave his girl waiting at the altar while he attended the daughter of a nestor was a pariah, no better than the sod-busters, who were home-steading on land that the ranchers thought was rightfully theirs.

Cliff returned to his office after a while and looked after his patient, who was far better than she had been the night before. Her powers of recuperation seemed to be strong. The sullenness had left her face. Rosa had fed her, combed the coppery mass of bright hair, and braided it for her. The yellow eyes were bright, and Cliff felt a little uncomfortable under the steadiness of her glance, for she did not take her eyes from him.

"There's lots of people in town, Doc," she said suddenly. "I've heard wagons and ponies comin' in since daybreak. What's the fiesta?"

"Your father's inquest, Shan." Cliff turned to look at her. "It's a matter of form, of course. An inquest is always held by the coroner after someone is killed. The facts brought out are then turned over to the grand jury for action."

"And who'll bury Dad?" she asked.

"The county will, unless someone comes forward with the necessary funds."

"I don't like that, Doc. Will you come here close for a minute? I got somethin' I want to tell you." When he was leaning over her, with his ear close to her lips, she whispered, "I've saved a little, Doc. I can't trust nobody else. You'll find it cached out by the Springs." In a husky whisper, she gave him instructions as to how to find the empty tobacco tin.

"You may need that more than he does, Shan," Cliff cautioned, "but I'll do it for you if you wish."

"Thanks, Doc." She put out her hand and gripped his fingers tightly. "You're a swell person. I'm mighty sorry I caused you so much trouble. And you'll go to the inquest and tell me what's decided?"

"Naturally, Shan. Don't you worry about it. And I'm sure the sheriff will find your mother and brother. Now, you follow Rosa's orders to the letter and get well as quick as you can."

Cliff went down the stairs to the street, strode through the crowd, and marched into the Mercantile, in the back room of which the inquest was to be held. Henry Rogers, the poker-faced merchant, was the coroner and undertaker for the community. Scanning the faces of the men assembled there, Monroe saw many that were familiar and some that were new. Pat Zanders, barrel-chested owner of the Squared X, who stood with Jim Croll. Kentucky Landers, who ramrodded the Circle Bar T for the estate of Percy Pim, deceased. Henry Scoles, the horse rancher, whose face resembled nothing so much as the mustangs that ranged his spread to the south. A goodly sprinkling of nestors and new settlers, most of them bearded, gaunt-faced men with a perpetually tired look about their eyes.

Again Cliff felt the glances of the ranchers, his old friends and acquaintances, narrowing on him speculatively. Only Kentucky Landers spoke to him—Kentucky, who had once been a puncher on his father's ranch in Texas.

Rogers called the meeting to order. Cliff was the first one called, for it was he who had discovered the body and brought the news to town. Plum followed, telling the condition of the homestead, but vouchsafing no guess as to who the killers might be.

The inquest lasted less than fifteen minutes. The jury brought in a verdict of death by person or persons unknown. It was what had been expected, but a tall, rangy settler took up the cudgel for the nestors by striding through the crowd and facing the sheriff.

"Just what you aimin' to do, lawman?" he demanded.

"What I'm supposed to do," Plum snapped back testily. "Find the killers and bring 'em to trial. I told you that, so far, there weren't no clues as to who done it. But I ain't got long to work. Come two days, a new lawman takes office. Maybe you'd better ask that question of Bonnett here."

In spite of his big body, the sheriff-elect was ill at ease in front of these men. He had seen too many range wars start with less provocation.

"You men elected me to uphold the law," he said grimly, "and I've taken oath to do it. I'll ride this range from hell to breakfast huntin' for the killers. And when I find 'em, they'll be brought in for trial."

Bonnett's simple declaration seemed to clear the atmosphere temporarily and to satisfy the tall hoeman. The men began to drift out again to the street, where they gathered in little knots.

Cliff followed them outside and strode back across the street to his office. No one spoke to him. Men turned their backs as he passed them. Word had been passed to each and every rancher, to each hired hand, that the medico was to be ostracized. They were doing just that, ignoring him to a point where he felt like flying into a rage, telling them all what he thought of them.

Shan saw the grimness of his face when he entered her room, and a look of pity came into her eyes. No one realized better than she the spot she had put him in.

Rosa came across the room and handed him a folded slip of paper. "A *señor* put thees beneath the door," she said.

Cliff took the paper, unfolded it, then suddenly clenched it in his fist. "Did you see the man, Rosa?" he queried grimly.

The Mexican woman shook her head. "No, *Señor* Doc. He ees come quietly. I have heard hees boots going pronto down the steps, but I have not seen heem. Eet ees *malo* news?"

Cliff nodded. "Mighty bad. You're going to have to keep your eyes open, Rosa. And you, too, Shan. It concerns you. Someone threatens to kidnap you and take you out of the county if I don't move you out. From now on, you'll sleep with a gun under your pillow. I've a shotgun there in the cupboard, Rosa. I'm sure you know how to use it, for I've seen you hunting prairie chickens. How about you, Shan? Can you handle a Colt?"

For the first time since she had been moved from the homestead to this place, Shan's mouth crescented and she laughed softly. "Just try me, Doc," she said. "I can bust the guts out of a gopher at twenty yards. And I'd sure like to do the same to the buzzard that comes coyotin' around here."

# CHAPTER FIVE

FOR several days after receipt of the warning, Cliff tried to get some clue to the identity of its sender, but without success. No one had seen anyone enter the medico's office during the inquest, for the very good reason that no one had been on the street. Nor could the new sheriff shed any light on the mystery.

"The gent ought to know that you don't scare easy," Bonnett said, "but, just the same, we'll keep a sharp eye on any of them that acts suspicious. This killin's got me plumb buffaloed. Me and Dorr been over the ground plenty thorough, and we ain't yet been able to cut a plain trail that 'ud lead to the dirty hombres that murdered Jungward. There weren't even a pony track, outside of yours. But what beats me is the disappearance of Mrs. Jungward and the button. It don't seem natural for the coyotes to take them two along with 'em. I wouldn't be a mite surprised but what we'd find their bodies hidden in some gulley or out in the desert. I'm a-goin' to comb that tomorrow."

Cliff was content to leave matters in the big lawman's hands, for he had witnessed in the past some of Bonnett's cleverness and grit in tracking down criminals. The medico knew that the sheriff would leave no stone unturned.

Shan Jungward's recuperative powers proved to be even greater than Cliff had expected. Within a week, he was forced to let her sit up. This complicated matters further, and he was obliged to find either new quarters for himself or for the three of them. The gunsmith, who, with his wife, occupied a small cottage on the outskirts of town, agreed to make a swap with him. Cliff felt that, as long as he had to keep Rosa to look after his patient, he might just as well kill two birds with one stone and set her up as his housekeeper as well. The Chinaman's food was not easily digestible, and its sameness was ruining his appetite. This, coupled with the solid wall of unfriendliness that the ranchers had set up, was fast making him morose and irritable.

The new arrangement gave Shan a room to herself; the Mexican woman had a bed in the tiny kitchen; and Cliff had the parlor of the little cottage for a combination office and sleeping room. Rosa kept the cottage spotlessly clean, for she liked living in town, and was delighted to leave the desert hovel where so much misfortune had beset her in the past.

Manuel, her son, who was now a black-haired, black-eyed stripling in his teens, came frequently to visit her. Jeffries, the new owner of the S Bar 8, had given the boy a flock of sheep to tend, and Manuel was proud of himself. Cliff felt no qualms about him, for the boy was loyal to the point of adoration. Cliff was sure that he could count on him in any emergency.

The new quarters, too, gave Shan a larger measure of protection against the person or persons who had threatened her. Just beyond the jail and the sheriff's office which faced it across the street, it was open to the manzanita-speckled mesa behind it, with plenty of yard around it that was devoid of any hiding places. A man would have a difficult time prowling close without being seen or heard, for there were neither gullies deep enough nor brush high enough to hide him.

Just after he moved, Cliff mounted his big roan and headed for the S 4 to pay a visit to the injured Whitey Snow. In spite of Jim Croll's threats, he felt that the puncher's leg needed attention. It had been a serious break, high, near the thigh, and the medico wanted to be sure that it was healing properly, and that the leg would not be shorter than the other after the splints were removed.

But the big rancher was in the yard when Cliff drew rein, and he barked out, "Nobody called for your services, Doc. You can stay right on that cayuse and head back the way you come. When Whitey needs a sawbones, I'll take him to Bremen."

It took a great deal of Cliff's self-control to hold back the anger that instantly whitened his face and made his grey eyes brittle. But he did, somehow, and with a crisp, "Suit yourself, Croll," he wheeled the pony and left the S 4 spread. He had no choice. The rancher footed the bills for his punchers, and was entitled to have the medical help he wished.

Never one to quit under fire, Cliff made further rounds of his patients that day among the cowmen and the sheep ranchers. At each spread he was met with the same or a similar rebuff. Henry Scoles' boils were worse, as the physician could plainly see, but the horse rancher refused to have them lanced. Pat Zanders at the Squared X was not quite so bitter, and was more polite; nevertheless, he was equally as firm in his statement that Cliff would get no further business from any of his family or hired hands.

It was the same story among the sheepmen. Mullaby had a daughter ill with measles, but he, too, refused to let the medico see the child. "Your string's played out in this county, Doc," he muttered waspishly. "If you had horse sense, you'd pack your warbag and get."

That day Cliff found that he had only two men whom he could call friends. These were Bonnett and Tim Roney of the Lone Deuce. Plum had moved out to his little spread north of the town, where he cooked his meals, kept to himself, and spent all his time looking after his rabbits. Cliff heard of his movements through Bonnett, who was a frequent visitor there to talk over county affairs.

"I finally found out what's ailin' the old mossyhorn, Cliff," he said. "He blames you for his ruckus with Maw. It seems he ain't had a word from her since she left, but the stage driver brought news that he'd heard from a cousin of his that Maw was cuttin' capers in El Paso and havin' the time of her life chaperonin' the gals. Nancy's got herself a new fella, too," he added, and his eyes narrowed on Cliff. "I figured you might like to know that."

Somehow, that did not affect Cliff as much as he had expected it would, and he wondered why. Although he did not realize it yet, Shan Jungward was slowly taking the place of Nancy in his heart. Her cheery greeting to him, as he came in tired from a long day's ride across the mesa, always buoyed him up. She had that power. She no longer made inquiries as to the fate of her mother, and seemed content to rest and fully regain her strength before she took the bit in her teeth.

At first, Cliff had cast around for some other place to move her, but it was difficult. No rancher's wife would aid, and the settlers to the north were too wrapped up in their own troubles to want to bother with her. And Shan, who had drooped at the news that he was going to find another home for her, had immediately shown a marked improvement when he had announced that he was going to let her stay with him until she was well enough to look out for herself.

She was still too weak from the ravages of the disease to do much more than putter around the house, and Rosa kept a sharp eye on her at all hours of the day, hovering around her like a hen mothering her chick.

When two weeks elapsed without any hint of the threat against her being carried out, Cliff relaxed his vigilance and allowed her to prowl around the garden in the yard.

His patients now were confined entirely to the nestors and the Mexican sheepherders and their families who lived on the desert's edge. None of these could afford to pay much for his services, and, in many cases, they could not pay at all. But he was still the county health officer and, as such, drawing down his salary. Jim Croll, who headed the county board, had not again asked for his resignation, and Cliff determined grimly that he would not force the issue. He figured that they were probably waiting until they found his successor.

Bonnett was frankly worried about conditions, and confided often in the medico. The cowmen and sheep ranchers were holding almost nightly meetings, to which the lawman was not invited, and it worried him. He felt as if he were sitting on a volcano that might erupt at any moment, with disastrous results. For the first time in years, the two factions had united in a common cause. Each day saw the arrival of some new settler who had detrained at Bremen, outfitted himself there, and driven himself and his family across the sixty miles of lush rangeland, to homestead on land as close to the Springs as possible.

The town itself had changed its complexion entirely. Flat-heeled hoemen were now a common sight on the street, and their women and children could be seen in the Mercantile. They were a grim-faced lot who knew their rights, and intended to fight for them if need be.

Minor disturbances often resulted from the mingling of the two factions. But Bonnett kept the peace on the street, and Tim Roney, hardheaded Irishman that he was, would stand for no nonsense in his saloon. The saloon keeper welcomed the new business, and when Pat Zanders threatened to take his trade elsewhere unless the sod-busters were excluded, Tim told him off in no uncertain terms.

"You can take your trade, and be damned to you. If you weren't such a hardheaded pack of fools, you'd realize that times is changing, and that you can't get nowhere by bullyin' the hoemen. They're here to stay, whether you ranchers like it or not. If you're smart, you'll pull in your horns and start workin' with 'em and helpin' 'em, instead of blowin' up like a mess of firecrackers on the Fourth of July."

"You've said your piece," Zanders bellowed back. "And if you're goin' to cater to the scum, then we'll boycott the Lone Deuce. Come on, men," he called to the punchers and sheepmen who had filled the place. "Any dump would be a better place to liquor up than this rat hole."

They walked out in a body that night, but it didn't worry Tim. The nearest saloon was in Bremen. After they cooled off, they would come back, for a cowman can go just so long without his snake poison. And, sure enough, the following Saturday, the Lone Deuce was again full of cowmen and woolly nurses.

Cliff was changing, too. The ranchers' unfriendliness no longer worried him; he had become accustomed to spending his evenings with his patient. Shan was a good listener, and never seemed to tire of his stories of his life in Texas and in medical school. She had had little opportunity for education, for her father had been one of those restless mortals who are continually looking for greener pastures and more fertile land to till.

Cliff had plenty of books for her to read—some of them dealing with medicine, others by well known authors of the time—and she read all of them from cover to cover, sometimes surprising him by the depth of her knowledge.

Her beauty was a thing that was a never-ending cause for astonishment. There seemed to be two sides to her. She could be as feminine and lovely as she could be the opposite. When the subject of the settlers was brought up, as it was frequently, she became as hard and brittle as chilled iron. She would break out in vituperation of the ranchers and the men who she thought had killed her father with a vehemence that would have done credit to a mule skinner.

"Easy, Shan," Cliff cautioned her once, with a shake of his head. "Nice women don't talk like that."

"And you think I'm nice?" she asked artfully, subsiding instantly.

"Nicest girl in the county," he answered, grinning. "But don't you get any ideas about me. I'm definitely on the shelf. I was badly burned once, and I have no desire to try it again. A doctor's got no right to have even a sweetheart."

"I don't see why not," she pouted. "And you can't blame me for tryin'. You're by far the best catch in these parts. I'm like the rangers. I always get my man."

"Well, this is one time when you won't," he answered sharply, but smilingly.

"We'll see about that."

He could not be angry with her. He was pleased that she thought so much of him, but it was not love that was responsible for his interest in her. If he had had a sister, he would have wanted her to be like this girl. She was so full of vitality, so gloriously alive. She no longer appeared to him like the girl he had first seen walking the town's streets, boldly flaunting her face and figure before the men of the mesa.

"You've changed, Shan," he said, "and I'm glad."

"For the better, I hope," she answered, and her glance leveled on his, probing the depth of his grey eyes, and not finding in them the thing she wanted to see.

"Decidedly for the better. You're finer looking than the girl I first saw in Painted Springs, and you're softer, more feminine. When you came here you were hard, sometimes brittle enough to crack. I must admit I didn't think much of you as a woman."

"And you think of me now—as a woman?" she asked hopefully, the faintest suggestion of a smile crescenting the pleasantly curving lips.

"There you go again," he chuckled, "twisting my words. And how else would I think of you?"

"Cliff!" she said suddenly, and her hand shot out to grip his fingers. "I'm loco, I know, but I can't help it. You're the only man that's ever treated me like a human bein', outside of my father. You've given up the woman you were to marry because of me. Maybe I've ruined your life. Do you think that means nothin' to me? Do you think I'm ungrateful? Cliff, I'm silly enough to want to die for you." Silver fringed her lids, and he could feel her hand tremble where it touched his. "I love you, Cliff. Not even you can change that."

For a moment he could not answer. He did not want to hurt her; yet, deep in his heart, he knew that he could never be to this girl what she wanted him to be.

"Shan," he said at last, "I don't think any man has ever been complimented more. But try to understand. What I've done for you I'd do for the poorest Mexican sheepherder. Healing the sick is my profession. And you haven't ruined my life. I stopped to set Whitey Snow's broken leg when I was due at the ceremony. I thought, of course, that my bride-to-be would understand. She knew that she was marrying a doctor." He stopped and took Shan's hand, running the palm of it over her slender shapely fingers.

"She was a fool!" the girl burst out.

"Not a fool, Shan. No!" he answered. "No one could ever accuse Nancy Starweather of being that. But she had a temper, and anger makes us do funny things sometimes. Still, I don't think she regrets it. If she had—"

"You haven't heard from her?" she asked softly.

He shook his head. "Not a word."

"But your friends, Cliff? The men who stood by you in the past?" She nodded her head knowingly. "I know all about you. You stopped the range war two years ago. You were mainly responsible for bringin' that outlaw Puff Gordon to justice. You faced him with guns. And now you have no friends, and it's my fault. Poke and Tim Roney are the only ones who will speak to you."

"You're forgetting the new settlers, Shan. I've made many new friends there."

"Friends!" she derided. "Those ain't the kind of friends that you want or should have. You're head and shoulders above them. I'm a nestor's daughter, Cliff. I know the breed better than you do. The first settlers here were pioneers, a fine race of people who reclaimed this land from the savages. My people weren't of the same stripe. We were failures where we come from. If it hadn't been for Clem, we would never have come here."

The name struck a responsive chord in his memory. Clem was the word she had used so often in her delirium. But he knew of no man by that name except Clem Jeffries, the sheep rancher.

"Who is this Clem?" he asked. "You spoke his name many times when you were sick. I thought perhaps he was a good friend."

He saw her eyes harden and narrow. "Clem?" she repeated, and then turned her glance away from him. "Oh, he was the railroad man who told us to move here. You wouldn't know him. He lives back in Missouri."

He was sure she was lying, but he made no effort to inquire further. It couldn't be Clem Jeffries, the rancher. The sheepman was already allied with the cowmen to drive the nestors out. He pulled his watch from his pocket and glanced at it.

"Time for bed, Shan," he announced.

"But not here," a voice barked softly in the back of him. Then, as Cliff started to turn, startled, the voice continued, "Don't turn around, Doc. I'll put a slug through your brisket if you do. Hunker to your feet, gal. You're comin' with me."

Cliff had no gun on him, and none within reach. For a split second he was tempted to whirl and try with his bare hands. But the intruder sensed that, and pressed the muzzle of his weapon in the medico's back, freezing him motionless.

"Get goin', gal. Pronto, if you don't want the sawbones' gizzard splattered over the carpet," the man rasped.

Cliff saw Shan get to her feet and move back from him. And then something collided with his head and exploded, filling his brain with fireworks. Through the dimming fog of his vanishing consciousness he heard the girl's scream and the booming blast of a gun.

# CHAPTER SIX

FLAT on his face on the floor, with crimson spilling from the wound in his head, the medico was unconscious of the fight that raged above him. The intruder had slammed the barrel of his weapon against the medico's skull, sending him into temporary oblivion. That blow had changed the half-sick Shan Jungward into a tigress.

Since the day the first warning note had been received, the girl had carried one of Cliff's heavy calibre weapons tucked in her blouse, and she did not hesitate to use it now, as she faced the barrel-bodied, masked man whose weapon was leveling at her, while his slitted eyes lined up the sights.

She threw herself aside, ripping the buttons from her blouse as she pulled the medico's Colt out, and thumbed the hammer back. The man's first bullet burned along her side, but his second buried itself in the floor when her weapon thundered. The slug caught him in the middle of his body and doubled him like a jackknife. For the space of a moment, when his knees buckled, she saw him trying to point his gun at her, but his eyes were swimming, and his arm did not have sufficient strength even to lift the weapon. With a gasping oath, he pitched forward and lay still, his legs twisted grotesquely beneath his heavy body.

For a second she stood there, breathing hard and glaring at him, no sympathy coloring the tawny yellow of her eyes. In spite of the nausea that was sweeping over her from the bullet burn along her ribs, she thumbed the hammer of the heavy weapon back, ready to give the man another blast of the gun if he so much as tried to raise a finger.

He didn't. Not even a tremor shook his body, and she finally dropped the hammer against the firing chamber and slipped the weapon back into her blouse. Blood dampened her waist, smearing out in a crimson circle. She gritted her teeth against the pain and hurried to the door. Frantically she tore it open, and her scream could be heard from one end of the town to the other, the echo of it eddying off between the false-fronted buildings.

As her cry died out, she heard the sudden strike of hoofs from the mesa behind the cottage. Once again she whipped the gun from her blouse and, running around the building's corner, unloosed a volley of shots at a lone rider who was momentarily silhouetted against the skyline.

The sheriff's office door burst open and Poke Bonnett came barging out into the night, his long-barreled weapon in his fist. The saloon's doors spilled men, all rushing at top speed.

Tim Roney came bulging from between the two buildings with a double-barreled shotgun gripped tight in his hairy fists. He had come out of the back entrance and raced down the alley as Shan's scream had reverberated, and was close behind the sheriff when the two reached the gate and pushed it open.

"What the matter, Colleen?" he cried.

But it was Bonnett who reached her in time to fold her in his arms as her knees weakened and she fainted. It was the big sheriff who picked her up and carried her inside the house.

Accustomed to working swiftly in emergencies, Bonnett found smelling salts among the medico's medicines, and gave both the physician and the girl a good whiff of them. Shan came back to consciousness first, and opened her eyes.

"Is the—Doc—all right?" she whispered huskily.

Cliff was stirring now; the fog that enveloped him was slowly lifting. Tim Roney helped him to a chair, found water, and began to clean the ugly wound on his scalp. By the time the medico could open his eyes and look hazily over the room's occupants, the saloon keeper had bandaged his head.

Shan told them what had happened. Bonnett turned the masked man over, removed the black bandana from his face, and studied the gorilla-like features. The man's eyes fluttered open, but they did not focus. He groaned twice, and then his eyes closed again.

Cliff, still rocky from the blow, staggered to his feet, found a flask of whiskey in his kit and helped himself to a generous shot. It steadied him; and then he saw the red dye on Shan's blouse. With a quick cry, he reached her side and ripped the waist down, exposing the livid crease left by the bullet.

He was still a little dazed, but his fingers were gentle as he applied salve to the wound and bandaged it. "You were born under a lucky star, Shan," he said grimly. "I guess you weren't destined to die by a bullet."

"What about this hombre, Cliff?" the sheriff asked. "Looks like the slug went clean through his vitals, but he's still alive."

"Lift him up here to the table," Cliff answered quickly. "I'll see what I can do."

"Lift him up, be damned!" Roney barked savagely. "Let the dirty polecat die."

"No, Tim. I don't work that way. Put him there on the table, and be easy with him. We want him alive. We want to know who gave him orders to do this."

"Sure you can handle it, Cliff?" the sheriff demanded anxiously. "That was a nasty swipe he gave you."

"Certainly I can," the physician answered shortly, holding his arms out in front of him. "Look at my hands. They're steady as a rock. I'm like Shan—I'm too tough to kill."

"Then I'll hightail it after the rest of them," Bonnett said quickly. "I'll trail them killers from here to breakfast and back."

Tim Roney shooed the curious away from the front door, told them all to go back to the Lone Deuce and have a drink on the house. "Git, now," he ordered. "Me and the Doc got a very delicate operation to perform, and we don't wish to be interrupted." The saloon keeper was swelling with pride over the part he was about to play in the drama. He re-entered the house and stood at the foot of the table, watching the physician as Cliff rolled up his sleeves, laid his instruments out on a clean towel and prepared to probe for the bullet.

"What can I do to help, Doc?" Roney asked.

"If you can stand the sight of blood, Tim," the medico answered quickly, "get around here by his head. Put this paper cone over his mouth, and drip a little of this liquid on to the cotton. But keep your own nose away from it," he added sharply, "or you'll be falling asleep yourself."

"What the devil is the stuff?" Roney asked, screwing his nose up at the odor. "Sure and it smells like some of that rot-gut whiskey that they sell in Bremen. I always did think that stuff 'ud put a man to sleep if he inhaled it."

"It's chloroform," Cliff answered. "Quit your jabbering now, and give him a whiff of it. He's out already, but with this he'll be out long enough so as not to feel the knife."

Cliff bared the man's chest and belly and started to work. Shan lay on the couch where the sheriff had deposited her, her head turned towards the light, her glance on the medico's back. She heard the sheriff's pony go thundering out of town, followed by the posse that he had hastily collected. Then a silence dropped over the town, a silence so complete that in it the scrape of the medico's scalpel on bone was plainly audible, as was the deep breathing of the now white-faced saloon proprietor.

Shan, watching, saw Roney swaying on his feet, and, fearing that he was about to collapse, she struggled to her feet and came softly across the room. "Go lie down a minute, Mr. Roney," she suggested. "I'll take your place."

"The devil you will," he retorted huskily. "Go back there to your bed, but just bring me a nip of the Doc's good whiskey 'fore you do. Sure and a drink 'ud help to get the smell of this pesky stuff out of my nose."

Cliff did not appear to hear either of them. He was bent double over the wounded man, and his fingers were working swiftly, suturing veins, probing deeper and deeper for the lead that he could not find. He was conscious neither of time nor of place. It was always like this when he had a surgeon's task to perform.

Shan brought the liquor, then took the bottle back after Roney had drunk from it. Smiling a little to herself, she turned to replace it, but instead emptied the contents into her own mouth. The stuff burned her throat and tongue, and she made a wry grimace, but it sent the blood pounding through her veins and gave her new strength. Suddenly remembering Rosa, she hurried to the kitchen.

The Mexican woman was there, tightly thonged to a straight-backed chair, with a gag in her mouth and a neckerchief tied around her eyes. Shan cut the bonds with a kitchen knife and released her, pressing her fingers to her lips and cautioning silence.

Muttering under her breath, Rosa shuffled after Shan as the girl led the way back to the office. There in the doorway they stopped, watching.

"Got it," Cliff announced suddenly, and straightened. "All right, Tim. Take the cone from his mouth now. He'll stay under long enough for me to get him sewed together again."

His quick glance focused on the figures of the two women in the doorway.

"Rosa," he snapped. "Put Shan to bed. Pronto!"

The Mexican woman knew better than to argue. The doctor's word was law in this house, so she gripped Shan's arm and pulled her into the bedroom. But Shan could not sleep. She could hear Cliff's voice in the next room, alternating with the muted tones of the saloon keeper.

Later, she heard Roney leave and Bonnett come in.

"I trailed him past the S Bar 8 through the Canyon Espectro," the sheriff said, "and out to the desert's edge. Lost the trail there. It was all trampled by Mullaby's sheep. A whole flock of them bedded down there for the night, and the herder swears he saw no one. Durned Mexicans!" he grumbled. "Never can get anything out of 'em except '*quien sabe.*' How's the bushwhackin' sidewinder?"

"He'll live to talk," the medico answered. "Take his head, Poke. I think he'll be a lot safer in jail than here. If his friends have any fear of his talking, they might try to rescue him."

Shan, lying quietly and listening, heard the door open and the tread of their feet down the walk as the two of them carried the still unconscious man across the street.

Her slim fingers gripped the bedclothes, and she stared up at the ceiling and muttered to herself, "Just as soon as I'm able, I'm goin' to get out of here. It's not right for me to stay any longer than necessary. I'll find a place somewheres. Maybe the settlers will listen to me. They need a leader."

Again she heard the medico's feet crunching on the gravel, then the sound of the door opening and closing. He sounded exhausted, for his steps dragged across the room. With a sudden grim determination, she pulled a wrapper about her and opened her door. Cliff was standing by the mirror over the washstand, examining the wound in his head.

"You'd better let me clean and rebandage that, Cliff," she said, and went towards him.

He turned and looked at her, and she saw that his face was white and drawn. He swayed on his feet and had to grip the stand's edge to steady himself.

"I can do it myself, Shan," he said gruffly. "You get back to bed."

She shook her head and crossed to his side, gripping his arm and gently but firmly forcing him to sit in the chair nearby. "I'm not goin' to bed until that wound is properly dressed," she said shortly. "So don't try and give me no orders. My side doesn't bother me, and I ain't got much faith in Roney's medical savvy."

He smiled up at her as she leaned over him, and let his high body relax in the chair. "All right, Shan," he sighed. "I guess this is one time when I'll have to give in to you. I'm mighty tired, and my head feels like the Apaches were holding a war dance on top of it."

He felt her fingers gently removing the crude bandages the saloon keeper had placed there, and he closed his eyes and gritted his teeth against the sudden sharp pains that shot through his scalp.

Shan had seen him bandage too many wounds not to know the correct procedure, and the books of his that she had read had given her a useful knowledge of the value of cauterizing and cleansing. She washed the blood away from the ugly looking gash that had laid his scalp bare to the bone, and cauterized it with the liquids she had seen him use.

"You'll have a nasty scar there if I don't take a few stitches," she said.

He put his hand out and touched her arm, smiling at her. “Okay, Doctor Jungward,” he whispered. “I’m in your hands. Bring that little case of needles over here and I’ll pick out the one to use.”

He threaded the needle with gut and handed it to her. “Now give me the mirror,” he said. “Take the first stitch just above the temple and work back from there. About five will do it.”

He winced as the sharp prong bit into his scalp, but there was no clumsiness about the way she completed the job. He could see when she had drawn the two layers of skin together that it was a thoroughly workmanlike job, and he complimented her.

“Perhaps you’ve missed your calling, Shan,” he said. “I couldn’t have done a better job myself.” His glance caught hers and held it.

“I think you squared things pretty well tonight, Shan,” he went on, as the silence lengthened between them. “You proved your mettle in more ways than one. Now I think you’d better go to bed.”

He stood up and took her firmly by the shoulders. She swayed against him, suddenly tired and wanting the comfort of his arms. The top of her bright head just reached his chin. Her soft arms moved upward to encircle his neck, and she pressed herself closer into the arms that instinctively left her shoulders to encircle her waist.

“I’m tired, Cliff,” she whispered. “And frightened. That man might have killed you tonight.” She turned her face up, and again their eyes met and held.

Cliff saw the full lips that were long and pleasantly curving and inviting. He was hungry for the companionship of a woman, hungrier than he had realized. Nancy’s kisses had been sweet, but the kiss of this woman in his arms was like nothing he had ever experienced. It made him dizzy, and for a long moment he forgot where he was or who she was.

"Cliff, my darling," she finally whispered, "I knew you loved me."

Her words broke the spell that had held him in thrall, and he pushed her gently away from him, holding her at arm's length. "I shouldn't have done that, Shan," he muttered hoarsely. "I've no right."

She did not answer. He saw her lips tighten as if in sudden pain, and she swayed a little, her eyelids drooping to hide the mischievous look that flamed in them. Cliff, thinking she was going to faint, lifted her in his arms and strode toward her room. Her head hung down over his arm, and the white column of her throat was close to his lips.

But when he stretched her out on the bed and began to tuck the blankets in about her, she sighed and smiled up at him. "You might at least kiss me good night," she pouted.

"So you were playing possum!" He blushed. "You're the limit, young lady, and just for that I won't do it."

Grinning, he turned out the light and closed the door behind him. He took off his clothes and climbed into his own bed. Something had to be done about that girl, he reflected. She was too much the siren to be sleeping under the same roof with him. He did not love her. That kiss had been just a natural, instinctive reaction to her beauty. Yet he could not turn her out to fend for herself. With no trace as yet of her mother and brother, and with her father dead, she was alone and helpless in a man's world. And the power she had to move men would surely lead her into a hell of her own making, unless a strong hand guided her. Yes, something would have to be done, and soon.

In her own room, Shan was thinking much the same thing. Deep in her heart, she had little hope of the medico's ever really falling in love with her. But Shan was not like her father. From some long dead ancestor she had inherited the will and the grit to carry on. And she had a grim duty to perform that she was determined to carry out to the bitter end, even if it meant her life. Shan had loved her father, and somehow, somewhere, in some manner, she was going to exact revenge for his death.

# CHAPTER SEVEN

BUT Shan could not get out of bed the next morning, nor would Cliff have allowed her to. The wound in her side was not dangerous, for it was nothing more than a deep burn across her ribs, but she was still weak from her illness, and the nervous energy she had expended in wounding the intruder had sapped her vitality. Cliff found her feverish and restless, and prescribed at least two days in bed under the watchful eye of Rosa.

When he questioned the Mexican woman about her experience of the night before, she could shed no light on the identity of the man or men who had bound and gagged her. They had come up noiselessly across the mesa, crawling on their hands and knees, taken her unawares, and gagged her before she could utter an outcry.

Bonnett and the medico combed the mesquite in back of the cottage thoroughly, but it did not add much to their knowledge. Two men had cached their mounts in a gulley that was some distance from the house and out of bullet range. From there they had sneaked forward until they had reached the rear entrance of the cottage and the white picket fence that surrounded it. Here one of the intruders had crouched while the other had stolen ahead under the protecting guns of his companion.

Satisfied that there was nothing further to be learned there, the sheriff and the physician marched across to the jail to interview the prisoner. They had no luck at the prison, either, for the man was delirious, and Cliff had to give him a hypodermic to quiet him.

"I've seen that buzzard some place," Bonnett said, with a shake of his bullet-like head, "but durned if I know where. Might be across the border, and again it might be somewheres else. I reckon I'll get Dorr to look him over. He's got a better head for faces and names than me."

Cliff had never seen the man before, and guessed that he had been hired from outside to accomplish what he had tried to do. He and Bonnett moved outdoors to the plank walk and stood there for a time, watching the riders who were coming into the town, many of them brought there by the news that the medico had been wounded and that an attempt had been made to kidnap the nestor's daughter.

Jim Croll and Clem Jeffries were two of these. They joined the sheriff and the medico to get first hand news of the affair, but still showed their unfriendliness toward Cliff in no uncertain manner. If the physician had not been curious as to their attitude, he would have walked away and left them to talk to Bonnett alone.

Shan's words the night before and her mention of the name Clem had made him suspicious of the sheepman, and his glance narrowed on Jeffries as he halted in front of the lawman and remarked:

"Seems like it's about time somethin' was done about that hoeman's daughter. She ain't no good, never was, and never will be."

Bonnett put his hand on the physician's arm, steadying and warning him, and his brown eyes took on the texture of polished agate as he rapped back at the sheepman, "Hold your tongue, Clem—or maybe you're spoilin' for trouble. And leave Miss Jungward out of this. She's still too sick to leave the Doc's care."

"If she's sick, I'm plumb loco," Jeffries snapped back. "She weren't too sick to put a slug through a man's belly. She'd ought to be thrown into jail for murder. 'Tain't safe in this town with that hellion loose, and her with a gun. First thing you know, she'll be dry-gulchin' some honest rancher."

"Not an honest one," Cliff rapped out, "but a crooked, sneaking rattler that ought to be killed. Maybe that's why you're worried, Jeffries. No man with a clear conscience should be afraid to walk these streets."

"Are you insinuatin' that I had a hand in the killin' of her paw?" the sheepman demanded truculently, his hand hovering over the butt of his holstered gun.

"The doc ain't insinuatin' nothin'," Bonnett interposed, "but it seems loco to me that you ranchers are all so dead set on gettin' that gal out of town. She seems like a right fine young woman to me, one that had ought to be helped instead of hindered. Bein' the daughter of a hoeman shouldn't make her an outcast. You were all homesteaders here in this county before you got your start. And there's many of you that got your beginnin's in ways that wouldn't stand close inspection. Folks that live in mud huts ought to be durned sure the first rain won't buckle the roof over 'em."

"All this augerin' is gettin' us no place," Croll growled. "What we're honin' to find out is: who's the hombre that busted into the Doc's home?"

"Your guess is as good as mine," the lawman answered flatly. "I ain't ever seen the cuss before, and neither has Doc. Go in and take a look at him, if you've a mind to. Right now he ain't a pretty sight, for that gal did a mighty good job on his gizzard."

"Will he live?" the sheepman asked, and Cliff, alert to every tone of the man's voice, thought he detected more than mere curiosity.

"He probably will," the physician answered with a shrug, but with his glance glued to Jeffries' face. "I found the slug, and it doesn't seem to have hit a vital part. I'd say that his chances of pulling through were better than even."

"Maybe we'd better take a look at him," Croll suggested.

The two ranchers filed inside, followed by the sheriff. Cliff remained on the walk, his shoulders to the wall, while he rolled a quirley and lit it. Painted Springs was livelier than usual for a weekday. Hoemen, sheepmen and punchers swelled the ranks of the idlers on the walks. But they did not mingle. Each faction gathered in litle groups of its own, discussing the night's fracas.

The big, bearded nestor who had stood up for the hoemen came across the street to the medico and asked, "Is Jungward's daughter all right?"

Cliff nodded. This was Harry Suter, one of the earliest of the homesteaders. The man's strength of purpose showed in the level grey of his eyes, in the wide sweep of his shoulders, in the calloused hands. Unlike the other hoemen, he wore no gunbelt and carried no weapon.

"Sure!" Cliff answered. "Shan's all right, Suter. Just a bullet crease along the ribs, but I'm keeping her in bed for a few days. The shock of last night and the after effects of the pneumonia have left her weak and a little feverish. It won't set her back more than a day or two. That girl has plenty of vitality."

"Could I see her?" the homesteader asked.

"Surely. Just go over and knock at the door. Tell Rosa I said it would be all right." The request struck him as strange, for the nestor had never shown any inclination to be friendly, but he could see no harm in it. Shan was well enough to receive callers, provided they did not upset her. "Just don't stay too long, Suter," he added, as the man turned to go. "I don't want her tired or excited."

Bonnett and the two ranchers came from the jail as Suter's big body vanished into the medico's cottage. Croll shook his head and remarked, "It sure beats me, Poke. I don't recollect ever seein' that hombre before."

"Me neither," Jeffries chimed in. "Only I sure regret he didn't do what he set out to do." His glance raked the medico's face as he said it.

Cliff felt like smashing his fist into the rancher's broad face. He had always disliked Clem Jeffries. There was something about the man that antagonized him. And the sheepman had grown more obnoxious each day since he had bought out the Starweather spread, thereby making himself not only the richest of the sheepmen, but a power in the community as well. Since the settlers had begun to swarm into the county, the cowmen, anxious for help against this new threat to their livelihood, had elected Jeffries to the county board. The man was now like a pouter pigeon, all swelled up with his new importance, and bullying all those who he thought beneath him.

He had never liked the medico, and was leaving no stone unturned to see that Cliff was removed from office. The only reason he had not been successful as yet was because no other physician had been found who would accept the position, and the cowmen, remembering how the medico had saved their cattle during the foot and mouth epidemic, how he had saved the lives of their children and hired hands during the smallpox scare, were reluctant to leave the county unguarded until a successor could be found.

The sheriff's glance, raking the street, saw Dorr Plum jogging into town on his sorrel pony, and he said, "Here comes Dorr now. Maybe he'll be able to place the cuss."

It was the first time Cliff had seen the ex-sheriff since the night Plum had told him he was through, and the physician's glance narrowed speculatively on the frock-coated figure of the lawman.

Plum's old eyes saw Cliff, and the medico saw him grip the reins of his mount a little tighter and swivel his glance away. He dropped from the pony, and tossed the reins over the animal's head to groundhitch him.

Cliff risked a rebuff, for this man had been his best friend. "Morning, Dorr!" he said.

For the space of a minute, the old lawman's glance raked the physician's face without the slightest trace of recognition; then, suddenly, a smile flickered at the corners of his eyes, and crescented upward from his lips over the high cheekbones.

"Mornin', Cliff," he said. "When in tarnation you comin' out to see my critters? Got a mess of beauties now. 'Nough to make you a fur-lined coat for the winter."

Cliff choked, and he felt his eyes swimming, but he managed a grin. "Why, I'll ride back with you today, Dorr," he said. "Soon as you're finished here in town."

It was the first break in the wall of unfriendiness that the ranchers had built up against him and, for the first time in days, Cliff really felt like singing. He grinned at Jeffries, who was scowling blackly, and marched down the street to the livery, where he saddled his roan and led him out to the street.

"You sure don't look like a gent that'd almost cashed in his chips," Shorty Weaver grumbled, eyeing him disapprovingly.

Cliff chuckled, and swung himself to the roan's back. "Better wipe that long look off your mug, Shorty," he warned, "or it may set that way." Then he spurred the pony and headed for his cottage.

When he came into the sick room, Suter had gone and Shan was smiling. Cliff felt pretty good himself. It was like old times to have Dorr Plum on speaking terms again. The medico thought more of the old lawman than he did of all the rest of the folks in the county put together.

"You look like you had some good news, Cliff," Shan said, with a trace of jealousy in her husky voice.

"I have," he smiled down at her. "Dorr's invited me to come out and see his rabbits."

"I'm glad, Cliff." Her smile widened, and her eyes shone. "And Harry Suter wants me to come out and live with him as soon as I'm able."

"With Suter?" Cliff was instantly sober. Not that there could be anything wrong with such an arrangement, and it would relieve him of the responsibility, but somehow or other it struck him as strange, and he wondered. Harry Suter did not impress him as the kind of a man who would take an orphaned girl into his home without some motive. He already had a wife and two growing children. Another mouth to feed would complicate matters further. Cliff had seen the nestor's spread. It was clean, and the man was a hard worker, but poverty had laid a heavy hand on the homestead.

"Anythin' wrong with that?" Shan asked. "I didn't tell him I would, but I figured it was white of him to ask me."

"Nothing wrong, no," Cliff answered, with a shrug. "You'll still have plenty of time to think it over. I have no intention of letting you go any place till you're strong."

"I'm beginnin' to think maybe you *do* like me a little," she murmured, with a dry laugh. "At least you don't seem to want me to leave, and, heaven knows, that suits me. If I left a hundred years from now it would be too soon. And I'm glad, Cliff, that Dorr is friendly again. I know what that means to you."

The medico joined the ex-sheriff on the street, and side by side they walked down the board walk to the Lone Deuce. Tim Roney's wise eyes narrowed on them. He brought out a bottle of his best, and when Dorr poured both drinks and lifted his glass to the physician's, a smile creased the bartender's lips, and he said:

"This drink's on the house, gents. When an old buzzard like you, Plum, has sense enough to bury the hatchet, maybe things ain't gone plumb to blazes."

"I was an old fool, Tim," Plum answered with a wry smile. "It seems as if Cliff, here, is the only man in the county that manages to keep a level head on his shoulders." He put his gnarled hand affectionately on the physician's arm. "Me and Cliff been through a lot of troubles together. No woman's worth the breakin' up of that friendship."

"Thanks, Dorr," Cliff muttered, choked up by the lawman's words. "I've got a feeling you and I are going to still ride the trail together. It does seem as if Brant County would never know real peace."

The two had a lot to talk over, and as they rode towards the ex-sheriff's little spread, that he had named The Rabbit's Foot, they unburdened themselves. Cliff was amazed at the rancher's progress. Plum had less than an acre of ground, nearly all of which was covered with tiers of boxes, and each box was filled with rabbits.

He had built a barn on one corner of the property, and in this he did his butchering and skinning of the animals. There were tied bundles of fur awaiting shipment on the next stage, and the carcasses of the animals hung in a shed to be smoked.

"Can't get many folks yet to cotton to the rabbit meat," the old lawman complained, "and until I do, most of the meat is wasted, and I can't make a heap of *dinero.* Some of the new settlers are takin' to it now. It's a heap better than chicken, as I'll prove to you."

They moved inside the one-story house that a carpenter had built for him out of logs and shakes. It was a comfortable dwelling, with a single bedroom and a living room that played the part of a diningroom as well. Plum started his meal, and in a few minutes Cliff could smell the savory odor of the cooking meat.

The ex-sheriff had spent too many days and nights on the trail and attended too many round-ups not to know the principles of cooking. He concocted a meal, including hot, flaky biscuits that would have put a professional camp cook to shame. The physician found the fried rabbit tender and delicious. Afterwards, the two old friends sat on the small veranda and talked as they smoked.

"You failin' in love with that nestor's daughter?" Plum asked suddenly, after a long silence.

Cliff reddened, but he laughed and shook his head. "Not a chance, Dorr. Shan's a fine woman, and will make someone a grand wife, but my interest is purely professional. In another week or two she's going to move out to Suter's place to live with them."

"That's good," the old lawman grunted. "I was a mite worried about you, son. She's got a pretty face, and a way with men. And often, when a man's down, he'll grasp at the first straw. I don't savvy what it is about the gal, but I got a feelin' she's goin' to cause a heap of trouble hereabouts."

"I've had the same feeling myself, Dorr," Cliff admitted.

"Heard anythin' from Nancy?" the ex-sheriff then asked.

"Not a word. And I haven't written. I think that was a mistake, Dorr. A physician's wife has tough sledding. She has to put up with a man who is gone at all hours of the day and night. What's happened is probably for the best."

Plum grunted agreement. "That goes double for me, Cliff. I reckon I'm too old a buzzard to be takin' a wife, after all these years of livin' alone. Maw's a fine woman, but she'd been tied too long to Paw. She's got a right now to want to stretch her wings again and try 'em out."

The strike of hoofs from the range turned both men's attention that way. They saw Bonnett's big gelding loping towards them, with the dust billowing up from his heels. The sheriff drew rein in front of them.

"That gent we got in the calaboose is talkin' sane again, Cliff," he announced. "It's about time we had a little palaver with him. If you two can break away for an hour or more, I'd like to have you both there."

"You're the sheriff of this county," Plum grumbled. "Why in tarnation can't you run things to suit yourself? I got rabbits to look after. I can't be gallivantin' around the county listenin' to owl-hooters squawk."

"All right," Bonnett answered, grinning widely. "I wouldn't want to take you away from your profession, Dorr. I just figgered you might be interested. But Cliff's got to come. The fella might have a relapse or somthin' 'fore I get through with him."

"Dang your mangy hide, Poke," Plum flung back at him. "Can't you take a joke? Think I'm goin' to miss what that jigger might spill? Besides, you don't know nothin' about up-to-date third degree methods. I know a few tricks that'll wring the truth out of that hombre."

Plum got his sorrel, and they started back for town, none of them aware of the chain of events that was to lead the three of them deeper and deeper into a morass of trouble from which they would have plenty of difficulty extricating themselves.

# CHAPTER EIGHT

ANYONE there with him?" Cliff asked, as the three men dismounted in front of the jail.

"Yeah," the lawman responded. "I got Shorty Weaver to watch things till I came back. By rights, we ought to have a jailer here, but the jail's been empty so long the county board hates to advance the *dinero* for a man. Course, I ain't overly worried about this jigger. He's too sick."

Plum said, "You should have a jailer just the same, Poke. If we'd had one durin' the last trouble, they'd never have shot that man through the heart."

"I made Shorty a proposition. For a little extra he'll handle both jobs, turnin' the livery over to that button that helps him when we've got a prisoner. And the county'll pay for it, too, if I have to strangle each member of the board and wring it out of 'em."

They marched down the corridor to the prisoner's cell, their high-heeled boots ringing on the cement floor. Bonnett unlocked the cell door, and the three of them entered. The prisoner did not move, but he made a grimace of pain, and pleaded:

"I'm dyin', Doc. Couldn't I have a little shot of red-eye to sort of deaden things?"

"Perhaps," Cliff answered, feeling his pulse. "We might do even better than that, provided you talk."

"I ain't talkin'," the man answered quickly.

"Suit yourself," Bonnett growled. "We just figgered you'd rather take a quick trip across the border than spend twenty years in Yuma. And you ain't dyin'. The Doc here says you'll pull through. That slug played the devil with your gizzard, but it failed to hit a vital spot. Ain't that right, Cliff?"

The physician nodded. "The sheriff's right, my friend. You'll save yourself a lot of trouble by talking. All we want to know is: who's in back of this? Who wants to get that girl out of the way?"

The prisoner's broad face was twisted with pain, but his eyes were clear now, and, as he turned his head to look up at them, his glance mocking.

"My name," he muttered, "is Smith, Jones, any name you want to call me. And I ain't got the slightest idea what you gents is talkin' about. And you can skip that red-eye, Doc. I've stood worse than this, and I ain't worried about Yuma. Go on and get out. I never did hone to lawmen."

The three men looked at each other, and Cliff shook his head. "I wouldn't try any third degree methods on him yet," he announced. "There's plenty of time for that. But I would call the grand jury into session and return an immediate indictment. The sooner we get him out of Painted Springs, the better."

They filed out, slamming the steel door shut. When they had reached the office, Bonnett said, "Someone's payin' that hombre plenty to keep his trap closed, and I'd give a lot to know who. How long 'fore you think we can really go to work on him, Cliff?"

"It will be at least two weeks before he can be moved with safety," the physician replied. "In the meanwhile, if the man in back of this fears that the prisoner will talk, he may try to either close his mouth for good or rescue him. I think your best bet is to pass the word out that your prisoner's beginning to weaken. Shorty Weaver has a powerful voice. Let the townspeople see you both going frequently to the jail, and let Shorty do the yelling for the prisoner. Make plenty of noise, so that it will sound like you are trying to beat the information out of him."

"I always said you was the smartest hombre in this county," Plum said admiringly. "We'll start to workin' that right now."

Bonnett called Shorty, and the little hostler grinned appreciatively as the plan was unfolded to him. Cliff left the two men there in the sheriff's office and returned across the street to his own diggings. He found one of the settler's wives, who was suffering from a minor ailment, waiting for him. Cliff prescribed the necessary medicine, talked with her, then saw her to the door. Just as he opened it, a screech from the jail made her tremble.

"Sakes alive!" she exclaimed. "What's goin' on at the jail? It sounds like they were murdering someone."

"Just some of the new sheriff's third degree methods," the physician answered, with a shrug. "They're trying to get some information out of the man who attempted to kidnap Shan Jungward."

Standing in the door of his cottage, Cliff's glance covered the street. People had come out of the Rogers Mercantile to stand and stare at the jail. Shorty Weaver's feigned scream of anguish had brought another group from the Lone Deuce—brought men and women out of all the buildings.

"Why, that's horrible," the woman choked. "They'll kill the poor man."

"They won't kill him," the medico answered, "but, from the sound of things, I imagine they are trying to beat some sense into his head."

Anger flooded the woman's face, and she hurried down the street to report what she had heard to her friends grouped in front of the Mercantile. Cliff saw their glances narrowing on the jail. Such brutality was unheard of. Lawmen were not supposed to beat their prisoners. Cliff saw a sheepman mount his horse and go galloping out of town towards the S Bar 8. One of Pat Zander's punchers, who had been in the store buying supplies for his boss, hurried from the Mercantile, swung himself to the seat of his buckboard, and whipped his team into instant action. The vehicle rolled south with the dust boiling up behind it.

Shan called to Cliff; grinning broadly, he went in to see her. The heart-rending screams from the jail had reached her ears, too, and she wanted an explanation.

"It's just a scheme to try and find out who wants to keep the man's mouth shut," Cliff explained.

Shan smiled up at him. "I'll bet that was your idea, Cliff," she said.

"I won't deny it," he answered, grinning down at her. "It may work, and then again it might bring a storm of locusts about our ears. Have you any idea, Shan, who might want you out of the way?"

She shook her head, but she did not meet his eyes, and he knew she was holding something back. However, he did not press her.

Coming out of his office on his way to the Springs to see one of his patients, he saw Bonnett and Plum leave the jail, shaking their heads. Plum lifted himself to his horse and jogged out of town, heading for home. Bonnett strolled across the street and entered the Lone Deuce.

The next day, Harry Suter paid Shan another call while Cliff was out. Each day for a week, the same heart-rending screams of pain came from the jail at about the same time. And each day, more and more men gathered in town to listen to them, including Croll and Jeffries, who, informed of what was going on, had come in to satisfy themselves. But they were not allowed to see the prisoner, much as they stormed and demanded admittance.

Croll was particularly vehement in his denunciation of the new sheriff's tactics, and the sheep rancher seconded him. There was some talk of having the prisoner moved to Bremen. Yet no attempt was made by anyone to break into the jail nor to harm the prisoner. Shorty Weaver, now the full time jailer, strutted around town, proud of the part he was playing, but keeping silent on what was happening inside the stone and steel barred building.

Cliff made daily visits there to examine the prisoner and to change the bandages. The man was recovering swiftly. The wound was healing, and there was no longer any danger of infection setting in.

But two weeks of these tactics failed to break down the prisoner's taciturnity. He grumbled at the noise, and laughed at the sheriff's efforts to make him talk. Bonnett was getting discouraged, too, and Shorty Weaver's voice was getting weaker. He was getting tired of his role, and the daily yelling had changed his normal speaking voice into a husky rasp.

So the three men finally met again in the lawman's office. Bonnett said, "Whoever the polecat is that's payin' this hombre, he don't seem in the least worried. We ain't gettin' nowheres."

Plum and the medico agreed with him. There was no need to carry on the farce any longer. It was decided to call the grand jury into immediate session, and have the man indicted for attempted kidnapping and murder. Zanders, Scoles, Croll, Jeffries and Mullaby were part of that jury. A verdict was brought in swiftly, but there was considerable surprise on most of the jury's faces when the prisoner was brought before them with no marks or bruises on either his face or his body.

The only two men who did not seem in the least amazed were Croll and Jeffries. Cliff noted this, and it made him wonder. He was positive that neither of the men had known what was going on, unless Weaver had talked, and that he doubted. The jailer had been unusually close-mouthed.

Within three days, the prisoner was brought to trial. The jury was composed of representatives from each faction—cowmen, sheepmen and settlers. Again the verdict was swift. The man was convicted and sentenced to Yuma for ten years, yet it did not worry him. Handcuffed to Bonnett, who had guarded him all through the trial, he grinned as they took him back to the jail to await transportation to the penitentiary.

The next morning Cliff saw him lifted into the stage, with the big sheriff beside him, and watched the coach roll out of town.

The medico, returning to his office, found Shan ready to leave. She was well now, and she had accepted Suter's offer to live out at his homestead.

"I'll ride out with you, Shan," he said. "I want to be sure that everything is all right."

She seemed glad of that, and together they walked across the street to the livery. Cliff roped the steel-dust stallion that he had bought from Scoles to give to his bride as a wedding present. No one had ridden him since that day. He threw his saddle to the animal's back and cinched it tight, leading the spirited animal out to the street. The youngster in his teens who had been helping Weaver take care of the stable brought the medico's roan out. Cliff put the new silver-studded black saddle that was part of the stallion's outfit on the roan's back and told Shan to ride him.

Then he lifted himself up on the stallion, tensing for the explosion he knew was bound to come. You can't leave a pony on pasture for three weeks without expecting trouble. It came suddenly, almost unseating him by its violence. Cliff could hear Shan's peals of laughter as the animal shot into the air, came down stiff-legged, and pivoted.

The sound of hoofs and the shrill neigh of the horse brought men running to witness the fun. Cliff did not care. He had helped to break the stallion to the saddle in the first place, for he had wanted to be sure it would be gentle enough for Nancy to ride.

"Ride 'em, Doc!" "Hold 'im, Sawbones." "He's sheddin' water." "Put glue on your seat!" These and other expressions of mockery or praise came from the throats of the punchers who were standing on the planked walk watching the stallion's gyrations.

But the fun did not last long. The steel-dust was only limbering up after his weeks of idleness. He settled down finally, stopped his bucking, and stood there, with his head arched proudly. Cliff wiped the sweat and dust from his face with his handkerchief and, grinning at the crowd, motioned to the girl to follow him. He reined the stallion around, and the two headed out of town at a fast lope.

Not until they had left Painted Springs far behind did he check the pony's speed and bring it to a walk. "I never rode a better bronc," he said, looking at Shan and smiling.

She nodded, but did not answer. Now that her sojourn in the medico's house had definitely come to an end, it depressed her.

They reached Suter's little spread, with its cabin of logs, its sahuaro pole corral, its barn whose roof sagged at a crazy angle. Chickens were scratching in the yard, and a pig went squealing around the corner of the house as they drew rein.

Suter's homestead was only a few miles from the Springs themselves. The jagged, cathedral-like upthrusts of red sandstone could be seen to the south, with the noonday sun making deep reservoirs of color out of the hollows and water-gutted depressions. The settler had picked a more fertile piece of land than Jan Jungward, and every foot of the ground had been tilled.

Cliff could see Mrs. Suter, dressed in worn Levis, working in the field at some distance from the house, but he could not see the nestor nor either of the two children.

Shan got down from the roan and stood by the animal's head, looking up at the medico. Her tawny eyes were shadowed by the wide brim of the hat she wore. Her copper hair had been clubbed into a thick knot at the base of her skull, and the sun, touching it, brought out all its brightness.

The physician was depressed now, too. Suter's homestead did not reflect the character of this girl. It was like placing a priceless ruby into a brassy setting. Straight and slim as a reed, she seemed utterly out of place in this poverty.

Trying not to show his feelings, Cliff dropped from the stallion's back and began loosening the cinch strap. Shan's eyes widened as she watched him lift his saddle from the pony's back, then move to the roan and do the same. He exchanged saddles first, and then bridles. When he had completed the change, he turned to Shan and said, embarrassed:

"The steel-dust is a sort of a going away present, Shan. He's yours now, saddle, bridle, and all, and I hope you get a lot of enjoyment out of him."

"Cliff!" Amazement and pleasure at the gift choked her voice. "But you mustn't do that," she added. "You bought that stallion for your—"

"My bride, yes—" he stopped her, his glance meeting hers, his lips crescenting. "But there was no bride, Shan, and the way I feel now, there never will be one. I want you to have him."

"That's swell, Cliff." She left the roan's head and moved towards him. "But how can I thank you? You've done so much for me."

Fearful of the look in her eyes, afraid that he might again take this girl in his arms, he edged around the stallion's flanks, putting the animal between them. He did not want thanks. He only wanted to get away, before the power of this girl broke through the wall of his reserve.

The roan was in back of him now, and, turning, he lifted himself to the saddle. "I hope you get a lot of pleasure out of him, Shan," he said. "He comes of fine stock, the best that Henry

Scoles' horse ranch could produce. And I don't want any thanks. My pleasure is in seeing you strong and healthy again. Take care of yourself, and always remember you can count on me as your friend."

For a long time she stood there by the stallion's proud head, watching the medico's broad back disappear across the mesa. "A friend," she lamented. "I don't want him for a friend. The fool!" And then, with a sudden grim set to her lips, she gripped the reins of the pony and lifted herself to his back.

Maida Suter, seeing the girl in front of the cabin, was hastening to bid her welcome, when suddenly she stopped in amazement and stared, wide-eyed. Shan Jungward was not waiting. She was spurring her horse towards the Springs. Even as the settler's wife watched, she saw pony and rider vanish between two of the upthrusting spires of sandstone.

# CHAPTER NINE

THE medico jogged on back to town, unaware of the girl's change of plans. And then he remembered something that he had forgotten, and he wheeled the roan, just as the buildings of Painted Springs swam into his vision. He had neglected to tell Shan that the money she had so carefully saved in the tobacco tin was still where she had hidden it. Cliff had not even hunted for the treasure. He had dipped into his own pocket to pay the burial expenses of her father.

The knowledge that he was going to see her again almost immediately buoyed him up, and he urged the roan to a faster gait. Somehow the sun seemed brighter now, and the cholla greener, and the spires of the Springs more colorful.

He brought the pony to an abrupt halt in front of Suter's cabin and dropped to the ground, calling Shan's name. But it was Maida Suter who came to the door, and his face turned sober.

"Where's Miss Jungward?" Cliff asked quickly. He had seen Mrs. Suter in town, but this was the first time he had ever spoken to her directly, and her glance, brittle as glass, was not friendly.

"You're the medico, aren't you?" she asked sharply. "Well, I might ask you the same question. I saw her here just after you'd left, and I came hurrying from the fields to welcome her. But she didn't stay. The last I saw of her, she was going through that gap over by the Springs, heading for heaven knows where. The ungrateful hussy! It does seem like she might be more polite, after what Harry's trying to do for her. I told him it was a crazy idea, bringing that girl here. I've got enough mouths to feed now, and enough trouble getting food for them. I hope she doesn't come. Good riddance, I say."

"Just a minute, Mrs. Suter," Cliff snapped back, when at last she stopped talking. "Haven't you any idea where she went? Didn't she speak to you at all?"

"Certainly not," the woman flared waspishly. "If she saw me at all, she pretended she didn't. And I hope she's gone for good. She's a brazen trollop, too pretty to be straight. Land sakes! Like the rest of the women in these parts, I was surprised that a fine man like you would defend her and take her into your home. You wouldn't have done it if you'd had a wife. I never wanted her here, I can tell you that—and if she comes now, I'll move out, bag and baggage."

"All right," the medico answered placatingly. "Perhaps you're right, Mrs. Suter. But I'm going to look for her." Before she could open her mouth and start afresh, he wheeled his pony and left her standing there, a high, grim figure against the dun-colored background of the cabin.

It was not fear that made him urge the roan to a fast gait, but anxiety as to Shan's plans. He knew of no place where she might go, and he didn't think the girl was foolish enough to try and cross the desert at this time of day without provisions. The stallion was fresh, and it would be possible for her to reach Coyote Wells by late night, provided she knew the trail. But why would she go there?

He reached the bubbling springs, where the clear water oozed from the ground, and stopped long enough for his pony to drink his fill. Waving willows and lush green grass surrounded the water hole. Even at this time of the year, when the rest of the mesa was dry and dun-colored, the carpet of green around the springs was sprinkled with buttercups and Johnnyjump-ups.

He walked the roan through the narrow gap; the spires of stone rose above him. It was a narrow trail, barely wide enough for a horse and rider. In some prehistoric era, a glacier had covered this land, flattening and leveling the surrounding terrain, but leaving these turrets and embattlements for the wind and rain to work upon. It was a short cut to the desert beyond, where the Mexican sheepherders lived, and the physician had traversed it many times in the past. It was perhaps a mile in depth at the base, with queer formations of rock upthrusting towards the blue sky. There were occasional solid walls of red-hued sandstone with deep fissures, whose depth could not be ascertained by casual observation.

Knowing the trail and the way the girl had come, Cliff did not bother to look for sign, for he knew that she could only go straight ahead. But when he reached the desert's edge, and there was no sign of a rider on its flat, mesquite-studded surface, he grew worried and turned to look back the way he had come.

Not far from where he stopped was the hovel of a sheepherder, a withered old Mexican, whom the medico had treated during the smallpox epidemic, and Cliff turned his mount that way. But the old man was not in, and the physician could see no sign of the small flock of woollies that he tended for Jeffries.

For an hour or more the medico rode back and forth along the edge of the desert, his glance probing the ground and searching for some sign of the girl's mount. Occasionally he would lift his eyes and stare out across the arid waste, hoping to get a glimpse of a rider.

Shaking his head finally in exasperation, he turned the roan's head toward home, heading back via the gap. Hemmed in by the water-etched walls, the ride was depressing, for the sun no longer touched the floor of the trail, and a breeze was rising that whistled eerily through the fissures.

It was useless now to look for sign, for he had already passed this way once, and the scrape of the roan's shod hoofs would have obliterated any marks of the stallion. Besides, there was no other way to go except straight through. Either Shan had cut south and had been hidden by these same peaks, or she had rounded them to the north. But the nearest town in that direction was more than a hundred miles away, and it did not seem likely she would have tried it.

Lights were cutting broad patterns across the dust of the street when he reached his house, hitched his pony to the picket fence and entered his office. A further pall of gloom struck him instantly. Shan had always met him or called to him from her sick room. Now there was no one. Cliff could not even hear the rattle of pots and pans from the kitchen, and he went there quickly, searching for Rosa.

The kitchen was empty and, from the looks of it, the Mexican woman had not planned any dinner for this night. Nor could the physician find any of her clothing hanging in the closet. It appeared that Rosa had left, too.

Cliff stifled an oath and went back to his office. But he could not stand the silence of the place, and finally, in desperation, he stalked across to the Lone Deuce.

It was a relief to find Tim Roney's jovial round face behind the mahogany. Here, at last, was a friend to whom he could unburden his troubles. With a drink in his hand, Cliff told the saloon keeper of Shan's disappearance.

"Can't blame her much for not wantin' to go to Suter's house," Roney said, with a wise shake of his head. "His old woman's a magpie, a hellion if I ever seen one. How Suter puts up with her is more than I can figger. The pesky female never seems to run down."

"But where would she go, Tim?" Cliff demanded.

The saloon keeper shook his head and leaned his elbows on the bar. "Sure and there is a riddle," he replied. "Now, if she'd headed south, I'd say she was goin' to Bremen. A smart girl with a pretty face could find plenty of work there, and Shan is both smart and pretty." His glance narrowed on the medico. "You wasn't by any chance fallin' in love with the colleen, was you, Doc?"

Cliff felt the color suffusing his face, but he laughed and shook his head. "I'm damned if I know, Tim," he answered. "I don't mind admitting that I miss her like the very devil. My house is like a morgue now."

"Humph! Love's a queer thing, Doc. It makes the world go 'round, but it don't make sense. Have another drink. There's nothin' like good whiskey to drown your sorrows in." And when the physician had helped himself from the bottle, Tim added, "I ain't one to stick my nose into things that don't concern me, but it seems like you should have kept her on at your home, in spite of what folks say. I've had a queer feelin' about that girl ever since the night she put a slug in that jigger's brisket, and I'm thinkin' you ain't seen the last of her, nor the county either."

"What do you mean?" Cliff's glance searched the Irishman's face.

"Just this," Roney said gruffly. "The ranchers have got a leader in either Jeffries or Croll. Jeffries, most likely. He's swellin' up with his new importance, and he'll make trouble. But the settlers have none. As the days go on, they increase in numbers. They're gobblin' up grazin' land that the ranchers feel is theirs. Sooner or later we're goin' to see trouble here that will make the last range war look like a two-man ruckus. And it's my belief that it will be Shan Jungward who will ramrod the nestors."

"Shan! You're joking, Tim. Shan's a girl. How could she hope to lead the hoemen, and why should they follow her? I think your good whiskey is going to your brain."

"The whiskey maybe it is," the saloon keeper replied sourly, "but 'tis good sense. That girl has the power to lead men, whether it's for good or evil. That's why the womenfolks are all against her. I've yet to see the man that wouldn't follow such a girl through hell."

The bat-wing doors swung open just then, and several punchers and sheepmen came into the saloon. The physician knew all of them by name, but he turned his back on them, refusing to acknowledge any acquaintanceship. These men were all part of the solid wall of unfriendliness that the ranchers had raised against him. Roney moved down the bar to administer to their wants. Cliff finished his drink, nodded to Roney, and left the place, quartering across to the Chinaman's for a bite to eat.

When he had eaten his fill, he came out and stood for a time watching the play of life along the dark street. More riders had come to town, and the evening's pleasures were beginning. Men passed him, as he stood there smoking, but none paid any attention. They seemed bent on their own amusements. Cliff felt like a lone wolf, standing there in the shadows, and, on sudden impulse, he returned to his office, unhitched his roan and lifted himself to the saddle. It was only a short ride to Plum's spread, and he headed that way, with the cool night breeze whipping against his face.

The ex-sheriff was sprawled in a rocking chair on his little porch. When he saw who his visitor was, he smiled a welcome. "Light and set, Cliff," he boomed out heartily. "I been lonely as all get-out today." His voice was cheerier than the physician had heard it in some time, and in an instant Cliff knew why, for Plum added, with a wide smile, "Had a letter from Maw today. She'll be home next week."

Cliff put his hand on the older man's shoulder and gripped it hard. "That's the best news I've heard in days, Dorr." He sat down on the top step and rolled himself a smoke, flicking a match into flame with his thumbnail. Then, remembering what had brought him there: "Shan's gone."

"So she finally moved out to Suter's! That's the place for her, Cliff. She's a mighty pretty gal, and a right smart one, but it weren't right for her to be bunkin' at your place."

"She's not at Suter's," Cliff answered sharply.

The old lawman leaned forward in his chair, instantly attentive. "Where did she go, then?"

"That's what I'd like to know." The medico shrugged his wide shoulders, and his glance narrowed on the distant, faint lights of the town. He told Plum of his trip to the settler's, of his return there to tell Shan of her hidden money, and of his subsequent ride to the desert's edge trying to catch up with her. "It seemed as if the earth had swallowed her up," he concluded. "Not a sign to cut, nothing to show where she might have turned off." He did not mention his gift of the stallion.

"What kind of a bronc was she ridin', and where did she get it?" Plum demanded.

A little sheepishly. Cliff told him of his gift of the steel-dust and the new saddle.

"I used to think there was no fool like an old one," the ex-sheriff growled, "but, son, you sure take first prize for generosity. Why, I'd 've given my right arm for that critter! You paid Hank Scoles three hundred for him, and the saddle and bridle must 've cost you near as much. No wonder the gal hightailed it. She was scared you might change your mind."

"I wanted her to have it, Dorr," Cliff replied, a little angered by the man, but not wanting to start an argument. "The girl's never had much chance."

A gun sounded from the direction of town, followed by another. Plum turned his chair and looked that way, then gritted,

"Now what in tarnation's goin' on? Bonnett's still away. Dag-nab it! I suppose I got to ride in there to keep the peace. That's the trouble with bein' a lawman, Cliff. Your job never ends, even when you resign. I'll get my sorrel, and we'll go in together."

It didn't take the ex-sheriff long. He jogged around the house, and the two headed for town. But no more gunfire broke the town's peace, and, as they rode down the main street, everything seemed to be peaceful.

"Just a little ruckus, most likely," the old lawman grunted, as he got stiffly off his horse and hitched him to the rail in front of the Lone Deuce. "Long as we're here, we might as well have a nightcap."

The physician followed him in. Much to their surprise, the saloon was empty. There was no one there but Roney, and he was busy wiping and polishing glasses. He turned and glared at them as they came in.

"Where is everybody?" Cliff asked.

"All gone to Jeffries' spread," Roney answered sharply; then, with a smothered curse, he took one of the glasses in his hand and savagely smashed it to the floor. "Why in blazes I ever went into business in this fool county is more than I've been able to figger out. The danged bullheaded fools is at it again. Hell's broke loose on the range tonight."

The medico had never seen the Irishman quite so angry and disgusted. His round face was red with rage, and his blue eyes glittered like the glass balls on a lampshade.

"Did you hear me?" he rasped out. "Some mangy pack of buzzards busted into the S Bar 8 spread tonight. They set Jeffries' house afire, touched a match to three of his haystacks, and tried to riddle the woolly nurses with bullets. There weren't no one hurt, but they sure started somethin'."

# CHAPTER TEN

FOR a long moment, the two men stood there staring at the saloon keeper. Plum's face was screwed up in disgust, and his teeth were locked tightly. He held the filled whiskey glass tight in his gnarled fingers. His faded blue eyes seemed almost to be looking straight through the bulky form of Roney. And then suddenly he brought the glass to his lips, drained the contents, and wiped his mouth with the back of his hand. A long sigh issued from his lips.

"And Poke still away on his trip to Yuma," he exclaimed disgustedly. "Once a lawman, always a lawman. I reckon I might as well go and get my guns, Cliff. Looks like I got to keep the peace in this county. You honin' to mix into it?" His glance swiveled around to concentrate on the sober face of the physician.

"I've got more reason than you, Dorr," Cliff replied quickly. "You're no longer the sheriff, but I'm still the county health officer. In the absence of Bonnett, I believe I am the next in authority. Besides, I think you're going to need some backing."

Plum's wrinkled face broke into a derisive grin, and he turned to Roney, remarking sardonically, "That's youth talkin', Tim. This danged medico's always stickin' his nose into things. And like the rest o' 'em hereabouts, he thinks I'm too old for sheriffin'." The smile left his face, and he added to Cliff, "Better get your gun. You may need powder smoke more than a tin badge to hold them hellions in line."

It was against the medico's rules to carry weapons, except in emergencies, and he failed to see what good a gun would do him against the undoubtedly hotheaded and vengeful ranchers, who were probably gathered by this time at the S Bar 8. However, he did not argue the point with the sheriff. Plum knew his business, and Cliff followed him out to the street.

While the old lawman was hurrying back to his own spread for his twin stag-butted weapons with their long-worn and polished barrels, Cliff marched to his office, found his gunbelt and buckled it on. It had been a good many months since he had worn the weapon, and it felt heavy along his thigh. He drew the gun from its sheath, twirled the cylinder and hefted it to get the feel of it again.

The swift tattoo of hoofs aroused him, and he hastily shoved the gun back into its holster and hurried to the street. Plum was just returning to town, his pace slowing as he neared the Lone Deuce. Cliff saw Plum's glance drop to the medico's thigh, saw him nod with satisfaction. Plum had seen Cliff use that weapon, and he knew that, regardless of what happened, the doctor would back him to the limit. These two old friends had faced gunfire before in trying to uphold the law of the land.

They rode silently out of town, each absorbed in his own bitter thoughts. Plum was thoroughly disgusted at the part he was about to play, for he had resigned from office intentionally. He was just beginning to enjoy the peace and solitude of his new existence. He had turned the reins over to Poke Bonnett willingly, secure in the knowledge that his successor was a capable and efficient law officer.

Cliff was thinking of the last time he and the old lawman had ridden together. Plum had almost lost his life, and the physician had received a bullet in the side that had laid him low for weeks. But that trouble, he reflected, had not been caused by the influx of settlers. Then it had been the sheepmen against the cowmen, with the cattle ranchers trying to keep their range from being overrun by the close-cropping woollies. Now these two factions had buried the hatchet, and united against a common foe who threatened them with ruin. The settlers were reaching this county daily. What had once been free grazing range was now land chopped up into small parcels by barbed wire.

New cabins and barns were springing up overnight and dotting the prairie. Every available acre close to the Springs and the creek that wound away from it had been homesteaded. Fields of timothy and grain patterned the ground. The ugly bare arms of windmills now studded the landscape, which had once been barren of everything except the candelabra-branched sahuaro trees and the thorny, reaching fingers of ocotillo or greasewood.

The arrival of the settlers had changed the town, too. Henry Rogers had arrived to open the Mercantile Store. Soon after, the Chinaman had opened his café in competition with the Mansion House. Every building along the main street was now occupied, and new ones were constantly under construction. Painted Springs was growing, and consequently suffering from growing pains.

The mist had thickened until it was now like a solid wall of dirty grey that enlarged and magnified many times the night noises of the range. Sheep at times seemed to be bleating underfoot, when, in reality, they were yards away from the two swiftly traveling riders.

"This is a fine night to be trailin' coyotes," Plum complained, and his voice echoed and eddied from the fog with startling clearness. "At the rate this mist is closin' in, we won't be able to see a foot in front of us."

Then, suddenly, they heard men's voices shouting to them, and a man cried out, "Rein in them broncs pronto or we'll salivate you."

Both men brought their mounts to an abrupt halt, and their narrowing, straining eyes saw three men materialize out of the thick mist, like shapeless, ghostly figures without substance. One of them was Kentucky Landers, who ramrodded the Pim spread, and the other two were S 4 punchers sent out here to watch for riders.

"Roney told us about the ruckus," Plum rapped out sharply. "We figgered that, as long as Bonnett was away, it was our duty to see if we could help."

"The old buzzard brought that meddlin' medico," one of Croll's S 4 waddies complained, as he recognized first the physician's big roan, and then the man himself.

"Maybe you ain't familiar with the law of this county," the ex-sheriff barked angrily, "but don't forget the medico wears a star, and he can throw the whole caboodle of you into the calaboose for disturbin' the peace. Where's Jeffries and the rest of 'em?"

"They're back at the ranch house," Landers answered stiffly.

Plum spurred his mount; the three men fell in beside them; and in that way they proceeded to a point where the lights from the S Bar 8 made a hazy glow through the mist, and outlined the long veranda of the ranch house. A red glow from the still smoldering haystacks colored the sky in back of the house.

Plum and the physician dropped from their mounts and stamped up to the main entrance. Here, beneath the wide awning of the porch, the fog did not reach, and the faces of all the men grouped there stood out in bold relief.

Cliff saw Jeffries' broad face twist into a snarl at the sight of him, but the man seemed to be strangely unmoved by the raid upon his property. It was Jim Croll, the tall, walrus-mustached rancher, who felt the blow most keenly.

Plum inquired as to the damage, and listened to the story of each man in turn. They did not question his authority. Dorr

Plum had been sheriff of this county too long. Cliff stood to one side, watching the play of emotions across their faces, studying particularly closely the sheep rancher, Clem Jeffries. The man seemed pleased rather than angered at the turn of events, although his tongue was loud in his condemnation of the raiders.

"Did you see any of 'em?" the old lawman asked. "Have you any idea which way they went?"

No one had. The mist had been too thick. The raiders had swooped down, fired the haystacks, flung burning brands to the roof of the ranch house and, with a volley of lead, had spurred off into the blackness.

"It was a pack of them new settlers," Croll growled harshly. "Ain't a doubt of it. Who else would want to do such a thing?"

Plum shook his head. "I ain't so sure of that," he said, gruffly. "Hoemen ain't got the guts to raid a place like this. Course, there might have been some nestors in the bunch, but you can bet your last dollar it was no hoeman that was leadin' 'em."

"You goin' to try trailin' 'em?" Jeffries demanded truculently.

The old lawman shook his head and smiled faintly. "I ain't the sheriff no longer, and it ain't my place to be even stickin' my nose in this. I reckon you'll have to wait until Poke gets back, unless you want to deputize someone in his place. Maybe you'll remember I've been recommendin' a deputy sheriff for this county for some time. The place is growin', and Poke has need of a man, though you men are too bullheaded and tight with the county's money to see it."

"How about the medico, here?" Croll asked waspishly. "Accordin' to the law, when the regular sheriff's off on duty, the medico is the next constituted authority. Seems to me like it's up to him to trail the varmints."

Cliff did not answer. He still stood with his back to one of the uprights, watching these men. Until now they had been unwilling even to let him act as the health officer. But now, with trouble stalking them, they turned to him, expecting him to do two jobs for the price of one. It made him smile.

Plum spoke for him. "Danged if you ain't the orneriest herd of longhorns I ever seen," he rapped out. "For the last month you've been hollerin' for the medico's scalp. Now you're hankerin' to have him police the county for you." He looked at the physician and grinned widely. "How about it, Cliff? You honin' to play sheriff?"

"On one condition," the medico answered, and his glance met and clashed with Jeffries'. "If you men will give me a free hand, and will follow my orders, I'll try. I'm a physician, not a lawman, and I've had little experience in tracking down criminals. But what I find out may strike close to some of you."

"What do you mean by that?" Jeffries barked, instantly angry.

"I told you once, Jeffries," the medico replied coldly, "that no man had need of walking our town's streets in fear as long as he had a clear conscience. As far as I'm concerned, you're all guilty until you're proved innocent. Every man here has an axe to grind. You, Croll, and you, Zanders. The settlers are taking your free range away from you. I can read the writing on the wall, even if you men are too dumb to see it."

The two cowmen's faces turned red with anger, and their eyes blazed like bonfires. Zanders took a step forward, his fists clenched. Croll's hand dropped instinctively to the butt of his holstered gun.

Cliff seemingly ignored their movements, although at the moment he was glad his own weapon was sitting snugly at his hip, the comfortable weight of it giving him courage to say what he wanted to say.

"Times are changing," he went on relentlessly, "and the picture I'm about to paint won't be pleasant. There will come a time, unless you men realize it and face it, when all this county will be fenced. Brant County is fertile, my friends. More fertile than the adjoining lands. And good soil is like a magnet that draws settlers. There is water here, too. An abundance of it. You would do well to make your peace with the hoemen before it is too late."

"Bah!" Jeffries rasped explosively.

"You sound a lot like one of the woollies you raise, Jeffries," Cliff mocked, "but I hope you're not going to act like them."

"What do you want us to do?" Croll demanded. "You've been talkin' like a fortune-teller, but you ain't told us nothin' we don't already know."

Cliff said, "I'll call a meeting of the settlers for tomorrow night. If you men will get together with them, discuss your troubles, parcel the land out, some of it for homesteading, some for grazing, we can avoid a bitter war that may well mean the utter destruction of all you have worked and slaved to build up."

"Danged if it don't sound like good sense," Croll ejaculated.

The physician, watching Jeffries, rather than the others, saw a crafty light gleam momentarily in his green-flecked eyes. But it was instantly hidden, and he seemed to be weighing the suggestion in his mind.

The Squared X owner, Pat Zanders, unclenched his big fists and looked at the medico speculatively. He, too, appeared to be mulling the matter over in his mind. Suddenly he nodded in the affirmative.

"Maybe it's worth a try, Jim," he said to Croll. "It can't do no harm, and it might do a world of good. I sure ain't hankerin' to have my barns burned, and my wife and children hurt."

The physician was pleased at Pat's response, but he was not so sure of the two sheepmen. Mullaby was scowling, and Jeffries did not seem to be in agreement in the least. Consequently, the latter's sudden speech surprised him.

"I think there's good horse sense in what the medico suggests," he announced. "You call the nestors in, and I'll see that all the sheepmen are there."

"Durned if you ain't gettin' religion," Plum exclaimed in a relieved voice. "I callate there won't be none of you that'll regret it. Doc knows most of the new settlers, and I reckon we can depend on him to gather the hoemen. And, Jim, you and Pat can see to it that all the cowmen are there."

A sudden yell from somewhere off in the thick mist distracted the attention of all of the men. They heard the swift strike of hoofs; then, suddenly, a Mexican sheepherder broke out of the fog and brought his burro to a halt in front of the veranda.

"*Señor* Mullaby," the man croaked in a frightened voice, "*el diablo,* he ride thees night. Out of thees meest come many hombres with guns. The sheep ees keeled before my eyes, and one of them he laugh like a *señorita.*"

Mullaby growled an oath and leaped from the veranda, gripping the Mexican's arms. "How many did they kill, Adan?" he demanded. "Which way were they headin'?"

Jeffries' raucous laugh drowned out the little Mexican's answer. "There's the answer, Medico," he gritted. "You call for a meetin', and the hoemen reply with burned haystacks and dead sheep. You goin' to stand by, Jim Croll, and see these damned sod-busters ramrod this county? I ain't. Sam! Tex!" he yelled to his foremen. "Round up the boys. We're ridin' tonight for nestor country. By God, we'll give them a taste of their own medicine!"

The old sheriff was quick to react. With a sweeping motion of his long arms, he ripped his twin guns from their holsters and, holding them waist high, leveled them at Jeffries and the two cowmen.

"You ain't ridin' no place tonight," he gritted, "unless it's to the calaboose. Call back your foremen, Clem. I'm holdin' the aces in this deck, an' I'm honin' to play 'em."

"Why, you crazy old coot!" the sheepman exploded wrathfully. "Are you hankerin' for a swift trip to Boot-Hill? Sam's gun's pointed right at your brisket. Besides which, you ain't the sheriff no more, and you can't arrest me. Drop those cutters, 'fore one of the boys lets daylight into you. And you, Doc, lift your hands shoulder high. I ain't takin' no chances with you, either."

Cliff's swift glance, swiveling around, saw guns in the hands of the two sheepmen who stood in the yard. They were out and leveled. Plum saw them, too, and let his own two weapons thud to the planking of the floor.

"All right, Mister Meddlin' Medico!"

The voice, behind Cliff, was that of the Croll puncher who had accosted them in the fog. The physician had no choice but to lift his hands. He felt his gun slide out of its holster.

Plum grated, "I always figured you for a wolf, Jeffries. Maybe I ain't got no authority to arrest you, but it won't be me that'll end up in Boot-Hill. You're all swelled up with your own importance and, one of these days, you're goin' to blow up like a toy balloon, only with less noise."

Jeffries did not answer, just laughed mockingly and stepped off the porch. Croll and Zanders followed him. But the S 4 puncher did not relax his vigilance. When Cliff sighed disgustedly, the man's voice barked from in back of him, "You two can make yourselves comfortable for a spell. You ain't either of you goin' no place, so you might as well take it easy and set."

# CHAPTER ELEVEN

AT THE moment, there was nothing for the two men to do but follow orders. Plum sprawled his body into a straight-backed chair, which he tilted back against the wall behind him. He found a stogie in his pocket, bit off the end, and lit it. His gunbelt lay on the floor where he had dropped it.

The puncher saw the ex-sheriff's glance drop that way and, with a tight grin, he reached over with his foot and kicked the two stag-handled weapons out of reach. That done, he returned to a position at the edge of the veranda, his high body leaning against one of the porch uprights.

Cliff relaxed on the top step, close by him, and stared moodily out into the thick curtain of mist. He could hear the strike of hoofs fading away into the blackness. Jeffries and his hastily organized raiders were heading for the Springs. There was no telling what this night might mean to the county. Someone had definitely aroused the settlers. Even now they might be striking at the Croll ranch, or Zander's spread, while those two ranchmen were burning and perhaps killing in the north.

It was the forced inaction that worried the physician. He hated to have to sit by, unable to strike a blow for peace. As his eyes swiveled upward to the long face of the S 4 puncher above him, he noticed that the man did not seem to relish his job, for he was fidgeting nervously, shifting from one foot to the other. His gun was held loosely in his hand.

"This is what we get for meddling, Dorr," Cliff remarked sourly. "If we'd used our heads, we'd have stayed in bed, instead of gallivanting around in the fog."

"I reckon you're right, Cliff," Plum answered. "This weather ain't good for a man what's troubled with rheumatism. The danged dampness eats right into your bones. How long you figure to keep us here, Slats?" he asked the lath-like puncher.

"Till the boss gets back," the waddy replied. "Course, we could move inside, where it's drier. Jeffries don't like visitors to his spread, but maybe he wouldn't object overly much under the circumstances."

The puncher's booted feet were at the physician's back and, leaning as he was against the upright, Cliff figured that it would not take much to upset the man. He shot a meaningful glance at the ex-sheriff, letting his eyes swivel back to Slats Farwell's feet. Plum winked one eye and took a deep puff of his stogie.

"It 'ud be a heap better inside," Plum nodded.

The puncher's attention was riveted momentarily on the ex-sheriff. It was the chance the physician had been waiting for. His arm swung in a wide arc; he twisted his body, got his hand in back of the waddy's legs, and jerked hard. Farwell's finger tightened on the trigger of his weapon and he swung the gun around, but he was off balance and the slug went wild, burying itself in the ground at the physician's feet. Slats did not get a chance to trigger a second time. Plum came out of his chair as if he had been catapulted, diving straight for the man, while Cliff wrapped both arms about the waddy's legs, throwing him heavily to the planked floor. It was only a matter of seconds before both men were on top of him, and the weapon had been twisted from his hand.

"Nice fellow," Cliff panted, as he twisted the waddys' arms in back of him. "You ought to be ashamed of yourself, Slats. That bullet might have killed me, and then what would this county do for a health officer?"

"Durned good riddance," Farwell gritted back. "And you two ain't heard the last of this yet."

"Neither have you, Slats," the ex-sheriff chimed in. "Get the rope off my sorrel, Cliff. We'll take this buzzard to the calaboose, and let him cool his heels."

They forced the man to his horse, and there tied him securely, binding his hands with thong to the horn. Cliff said, "Maybe we ought to leave him here, Dorr. We haven't got much time to spare if we want to warn the settlers."

"Not by a jugful," Plum answered bitterly. "This jigger's too ornery to let loose. He might get away and warn Jeffries." He picked his gunbelt from the floor and buckled it around his waist. "Where do you figger they'll strike for first, Cliff?"

"Suter's, probably," the physician answered, lifting himself to the saddle. "That's the nearest to the Springs, and the first homestead in their path. I don't think they headed through town, and it will be slow moving through this mist. We can drop Slats with Shorty at the jail, and maybe beat them there."

The mist was still like a solid wall as the three kneed their ponies into it and started for town at a swift gait. They could not see a foot ahead of them, and had to give the mounts their heads, trusting to the animals' sure instinct to take them to Painted Springs.

Slats growled and grumbled with each beat of his pony's hoofs, threatening all sorts of misfortunes to both the ex-sheriff and the physician, until they reached the town's main street, where the lights were dim and blurred ahead of them.

Plum dismounted at the jail, shoving the puncher ahead of him. In just a moment the physician heard him talking to Shorty Weaver, and then the solid clang of the steel cell door rang out, and the ex-sheriff was again on the street, lifting himself to his sorrel's back.

Keeping their mounts close to each other, the two men thundered out of town, and on to the gently rising slope of the prairie.

Eventually they reached the charred ruins of the Jungward spread, and reined in to listen. They could hear nothing.

"Do you reckon we beat 'em here?" Plum asked.

"I hope so," the medico answered, shrugging, "but there's only one way to find out, and that's to keep on."

Once again they kneed their mounts ahead. Suter's homestead was not more than a mile off now; they could follow the newly fenced section that led toward it. Then, suddenly, the dark barn loomed ahead, and they could see the settler's cabin. No light showed, and Cliff called Suter's name as they drew rein in front of it. There was no answer, nor did anyone reply to his insistent knocking on the door.

"Look inside, Cliff," Plum suggested. "Maybe we're too late."

The physician pushed the door open and struck a match to examine the gloomy interior. The cabin was empty, and it was plainly evident that Suter and his family had left in a hurry, for some of their belongings were scattered on the floor, and the stove was still warm to the touch.

The physician turned out again into the night, puzzled by what he had seen. "Either we're too late, or someone has warned him," he said. "And if that's the case, we're wasting our time."

Plum held up his hand for silence. Both men turned their attention toward the Springs, their glances straining to pierce the heavy mist. Faintly at first, they heard the swift strike of hoofs.

"That's them," Plum whispered hoarsely. He dropped from his mount, took the reins of both animals, and made haste to move them around the cabin and out of sight.

Cliff followed him. They crouched behind a big rain barrel and waited. It was only a matter of minutes before ghostly shapes materialized out of the mist, coming to a halt in front of the cabin. Jeffries' bitter voice cut through the night:

"All right, Suter. Come out with your hands high. We want a word with you."

When no answer came from the cabin's interior, Jeffries gave swift orders to the other men to surround the building. Two punchers went past Cliff and Plum, but did not see them. Jeffries dropped from his mount and stamped toward the front entrance.

"How many do you see, Cliff?" the ex-sheriff whispered.

"Looks like six of them," the medico whispered back. "Got any ideas?"

"If they go into the cabin," Plum answered with a grin, "we could maybe trap 'em there. I'd sure like to get the drop on 'em."

Now Jeffries, who had entered the cabin, called to Croll and Zanders. The two ranchers dismounted and marched into the shack. A light suddenly blazed from the interior. Puzzled by the place's desertion, the three men were talking it over.

"Looks like somebody warned 'em," Plum and Cliff heard the sheepmen rant wrathfully. "Either that, or Suter's one of the men that tried to burn my spread tonight. I reckon we might as well spill the coal oil out of the lamp and set the place afire."

Croll's deeper voice was heard. "It won't do any good to burn the place, Clem. It'd be smarter to wait here till he comes back, and catch him red-handed."

"I ain't spendin' the night hidin' in this dump," the sheepman responded disgustedly. "Most likely he won't be back 'fore sunup. I'm goin' to set fire to the place."

There was further argument; the sheepman seemed to be the leader. The two men who had passed the ex-sheriff and the physician in the darkness now came from the other side of the house and stamped inside to report that the barn was empty and that even the stock had been removed.

"That means he wasn't figurin' to come back for a spell," Jeffries growled.

The talk brought the other man from the outside. Cliff saw him drop to the ground, throw the reins over his mount's head and walk up the steps.

"They're all inside now, Dorr," Cliff whispered. "We'll never get a better chance."

Side by side, the two crept from behind the shelter of the rain barrel. They moved away from the cabin and out into the blackness until they had reached the ponies, one of which neighed and flung up his head. Plum let out a wild Comanche yell, and Cliff drove two swift shots at a man in the door whose back was plainly outlined, putting the slugs into the thick logs, one on each side of him.

The sudden blast of the guns, coupled with the stampeding of the horses, brought consternation to the ranks of the men inside. The man in the doorway threw himself inside, head first, and the thick door was instantly slammed shut. Glass tinkled as someone shoved his gun through a window and let loose with a volley of shots.

Croll stopped him, yelling, "Do you want to kill the horses?"

The light winked out, and Cliff and the ex-sheriff, lying flat on their stomachs outside in the blackness, chuckled.

"That worked," Plum whispered. "We sure have got them buzzards bottled up and ready for the cleanin'. They ain't got no idea who's out here nor how many. And we're aimin' to keep 'em thataway for a spell. You watch the front, Cliff. I'll snake around to the back and put a slug or two into the logs at the rear, just to make 'em think there's plenty of us."

There was a few minutes' silence while Plum edged around to the rear. Then a gun laid a spanging sheet of sound over the prairie, and it was answered instantly by another volley. The ex-sheriff came cat-footing back to where the medico lay flat.

"Now we'll let 'em stew in their own juice for a while," he remarked.

From the cabin, the two could hear muttered voices and words that were indistinguishable. Lying flat on the cold, damp ground was not particularly pleasant for the old sheriff, and he complained frequently of the aches in his joints.

The silence lengthened. If anything, the fog seemed to thicken and the night to grow blacker. Somewhere in the darkness behind them, the two men could hear the occasional clink of a bit chain and, at times, the muffled movement of a horse. The raiders' ponies had not gone far. They were out there grazing.

It seemed hours before Croll's voice called out: "We only came here to see Suter and talk to him. If he's out there, tell him to come forward, or we'll burn this place to the ground."

"That's an empty threat," Plum whispered with a grim smile. "How in tarnation can they do that without gettin' their own skins singed? Don't answer 'em yet. Wait till they open that door; then we'll put the fear of God and the law into the salty jiggers."

When no one answered, Plum and the medico heard Pat Zanders exclaim angrily, "Durned if I'm a-goin' to spend the night here. My wife'll have the law out huntin' me, if I don't come home soon. I'm goin' out with my hands up. If them polecats out there is low enough to shoot a man down in cold blood, then they're a lower form of life than anythin' I've seen yet."

The door opened, and for a moment a hazy figure was dimly outlined there. Plum's gun barked, the noise of it eddying off towards the spires of the Springs. The bullet made a pinging noise as it bit into the mud between two of the logs. With a rasping oath, Zanders flung himself away from the door, which someone kicked shut behind him.

A string of epithets followed that blistered the night.

"Not bad cussin' for a God-fearin' man," the old sheriff remarked. "I reckon we might as well hightail it out of here now. None of 'em 'll try that again for a spell, and I'm thinkin' we've taken most of the fight out of 'em. They'll stay holed up there till it's light enough to see and, in the meanwhile, you and me can be rolled in our blankets, sleepin' peacefully."

The physician was more than agreeable. It was far from pleasant out there, with the mist swirling around them. They climbed to their feet and slipped around the cabin to their ponies. They took the reins and, walking softly, moved away from the cabin. Not until they were a good quarter of a mile away did they climb to the animals' backs and head for home.

Plum was thoroughly pleased with the night's work, and he chuckled and laughed all the way to town. "I'd sure like to see their faces when the sun comes up and they see there ain't no one there at all," he remarked. "And we'll keep this under our hats, Cliff. It might cause a heap of trouble if they thought it was you and me that had 'em cached there."

The physician left the old sheriff at his place and jogged on alone into town. There was still a light in the Lone Deuce and, after he had turned his roan into the stable, he marched into the saloon. Roney was asleep by his counter, and the place was empty.

"Where in tarnation you been?" the saloon keeper demanded, as he opened his eyes and saw the grinning physician standing by his bar. "You been out to Jeffries' place all this time?"

The story was too good to keep, so Cliff told him what had happened. "You'd better stay open till sunup, Tim," he finished. "They'll probably be a little thirsty and mad, and in need of a drink to revive their spirits."

Roney chuckled, but his face sobered quickly as he remembered a message he had been asked to deliver to the medico when next he saw him. "You had a caller tonight," he said. "That Jungward gal was lookin' for you. If you ain't been to your office, it's likely she's still there. She came into town about an hour after you and Dorr went hightailin' it for the S Bar 8. And she seemed mighty upset about somethin'."

The physician did not take the drink he had poured for himself. He hurried out into the night, and with swift strides covered the distance between the saloon and his home. No light showed there, and his heart sank, for he figured that Shan would hardly wait in the dark.

He pushed the door open and entered. Instantly a gun was pressed into his ribs, and Shan's voice, cold and menacing, rapped out at him, "Lift your hands, Cliff. I ain't goin' to hurt you, but I ain't takin' chances, either."

As the medico obeyed orders, he felt his gun jerked from the holster, and then he heard other steps in the room besides the girl's. "What is this, Shan?" he demanded angrily. "It isn't necessary to push a gun in my ribs."

# CHAPTER TWELVE

BUT at Suter's homestead, the six men locked in the close confines of the little cabin were about ready to fly at each other's throats. Their tempers were short and their nerves jumpy. The sheriff's quick shots had convinced them that they did not have a chance against the men who had trapped them here.

Croll and Zanders, with their two punchers, were in the majority, and they blamed Jeffries and Mullaby for their present predicament.

"It was a loco idea, us comin' here," the big S 4 rancher growled. "I'd ought to have had sense enough not to go followin' a sheepman. How do we know the men that killed the sheep and tried to burn your place ain't right now doin' the same to the Squared X and my spread? And here we set, unable to do a durned thing. Maybe there won't be none of us even get out of here alive."

"How could they be both places at the same time?" Jeffries retorted hotly. "My guess is that the whole pack of coyotes is spread around the house, just waitin' for us to show our faces."

"And they've got a right to shoot us, too," Zanders pointed out gloomily. "We're trespassin', accordin' to the law. We ain't got no right to be here."

"Nor did they have any right to kill my sheep," Mullaby grated, "but they did. I reckon if they can do that, I can hole up in one of their stinkin' cabins."

"I was against this business from the first," Croll grumbled. "The saw-bones had the right idea. What if Mullaby did lose a few sheep? That's a heap better than another range war. I callate you sheepmen have forgotten the last one, and the fact that it was the medico that stopped it finally. I ain't been able to figure you, Clem. You used to be a right peaceful rancher, till you bought out the S Bar 8. Now you're rantin' and honin' to own the whole mesa, it seems like."

Jeffries growled something under his breath that was unintelligible. Mullaby kept quiet. At the moment, he was inclined to feel somewhat the same way about his neighbor, Jeffries.

Zander's complaining voice struck out at them all, and his hand made a slapping noise as he struck at something in the blackness. "We've got company here," he yelped. "This place is crawlin' with bugs."

"You ain't tellin' me nothin'," one of the punchers echoed with a bitter laugh. "I'm already durn near chewed to pieces. I don't know what the pesky things is, but they sure do take a healthy chaw at a man."

Mullaby gave a snort of derision. "Ain't you ever heard or seen bedbugs? Nestors most generally have 'em. They stick to the schooners, and move right along wherever they go."

"Bedbugs!" The Squared X owner's voice rose to a howl of dismay. "Gawd Awmighty! You think I want to take them critters home to the missus? She'll skin me alive. Why, we ain't never had one of them durn things in the house!"

"Well, you'll have 'em now," the sheep rancher retorted, with a dry laugh. "You'll be takin' 'em home with you, 'less you burn your clothes and go home in a barrel."

A match flamed in the darkness, and for an instant all of their pinched faces were plainly outlined by its flickering light.

Jeffries cursed the puncher who had lighted the match. "You honin' for a slug through your gizzard?" he growled savagely.

"Even a slug through the innards 'd feel better than these meat-eatin' critters," the puncher responded disgustedly. "How long have we got to hide here like rats in a trap? I want a smoke."

The sheepman clambered to his feet and moved stealthily across the room to the window. He pulled the burlap curtain aside and peered out into the night.

"Ain't a sign of anyone out there," he announced. "Who wants to try and make a break for it?"

"You go first, Clem," Zanders suggested mockingly. "If they don't hit you, the rest of us'll follow. Me, I ain't showin' myself in that door till it's light enough to see. I'll take bedbugs in preference to bullets any day. The jigger that triggered at me knew how to shoot, and he wasn't foolin'. The only thing I can't figure out is why he didn't put a slug in my back."

Croll said, "We might as well wait until it's light. There's a mite of grey showin' over there to the east, and I figure it won't be long 'fore the fog'll lift. Then we can see what to shoot at."

This struck them all as good common sense, and once again they settled back into their places, with no sound except the occasional curse of the bug-infested puncher or the slap of his hand against his Levis. But each hour made their tempers shorter, as each man nursed his own bitter thoughts. The four cattlemen were becoming madder and madder at the two sheepmen who had led them into this trap. Both Croll and Zanders blamed Jeffries, and both had made up their minds that the sheepman was just what they had always thought him, a swelled up woolly nurse, and running true to the breed.

"What's that?" Croll whispered suddenly in the darkness, after what seemed like hours of silence.

The clink of a bit chain reached them, and then the muted strike of hoofs close to the cabin. Three of the men crowded to the window. The fog had not yet lifted, but it was lighter grey now, and objects were more readily discernible.

"That's my bronc," one of the punchers exclaimed in surprise. "See the blaze on his face?"

Now they all crowded around the window, their eyes straining to pierce the grey blanket that hung like a thick curtain around the cabin. The horse had come close to the log walls, and was contentedly grazing at the greener shoots of grass beneath the eaves of the cabin.

"Maybe this is a trick," Jeffries growled. "Maybe they put him there for bait, tryin' to get us to come out where they can shoot us down."

"Nonsense," Croll ranted. "I don't think there's anyone out there. Look, the fog is liftin'! Doggone it! There ain't a soul there. And there's my pony out there, too, and yours, Pat. Just as we left 'em. See, the reins is trailin' over their heads." He scratched his head reflectively and looked puzzled. "This beats me. You don't suppose them jiggers has hightailed it, do you?"

"Well, I'm a-goin' to find out," the tall, yello-whaired puncher exclaimed. "I ain't stayin' in this place any longer than I have to. I'm chawed to pieces by them bugs."

In a few quick strides he reached the thick door, pulled the heavy bar back and swung it open, stepping quickly back, with his gun palmed, waiting for lead to sing past him. Then, when nothing happened, he moved stealthily out to the veranda, and in an instant was swallowed up in the mist.

A few minutes later his voice reached the men hunkered in the cabin. "There ain't no one here. Come on out, you buzzards. Here's the broncs."

The rest of them made swift tracks out of the cabin. But Jeffries, once he was convinced that there was no one to molest them, turned back towards it.

"I'm goin' to burn this bug-palace down 'fore I leave," he grated.

"You ain't goin' to burn nothin' down," Croll growled at him. "I've learned my lesson this night, even if you ain't. I'll put a slug through your brisket if you try it. Get on your horse, Clem, and let's hightail it to town. Me, I'm needin' a drink bad."

The sheep rancher growled a protest, but it was five to one against his suggestion, and he knew Jim Croll to be a man of his word. Still grumbling, he caught his horse and lifted himself to the saddle.

Taking to the cowman's suggestion, they loped into the town and barged into the Lone Deuce. The sun was not yet up, but Roney, awakened by the medico some hours before and unable to sleep any longer, was busy wiping his bar and getting things in shape for the day's business.

"Mornin', gents," he beamed at them. "Ridin' early, or is this the end of the trail?" He saw the marks of the bugs on Canary Flack's long face, and a wide grin creased his lips. "What female's been clawin' you, Canary?" he asked.

"Cut the comedy," the big puncher growled back, "and set 'em up."

Croll looked at the saloon keeper suspiciously. Roney seemed to be the possessor of an unusually large amount of good humor for such an early hour.

"You act like the cat that ate the canary," the cowman gritted. "What in tarnation's the joke?"

"You think I'd eat that big gorilla?" Roney replied, his glance leveling on the big, yellow-haired Squared X puncher. "Shaw now, Jim. That 'ud be too tough eatin' for my store teeth. I was just thinkin' what a funny sight it was to see all you rannies this early in the mornin', and all of you scratchin' like you had the seven year itch. Didn't fall into a mess of ants, did you? All of you except Mullaby seem to be pretty well chawed up."

Jeffries glared at him, but he did not answer. He poured himself a drink, then passed the bottle on down the bar to the rest of them. Croll tipped his glass to his lips, while his glance continued to concentrate in speculation on the saloon keeper.

"What time does the Chink open up?" Canary asked.

"About six, usually," Roney replied. "But if you men are hungry, go wake him up. That tightfisted Celestial ain't never been known to turn any business down." He took out his watch and glanced at it. "Most that time, now," he added.

"Doggone, but I sure wish Maw Blane'd come home," Zanders grumbled. "We used to get some real vittles there. I never did cotton to this fancy food that the Chink puts out."

"She's comin' home," the saloon keeper announced. "Dorr had a letter from her. Them city fellers wore her out in El Paso."

"When?" Croll demanded.

Roney shook his head. "Dorr figured in maybe a week, but no one can tell about Maw. She's likely to come bustin' in on the next stage, once she makes up her mind to it."

The six men filed out, but the two sheepmen, conscious of the animosity of the cowmen and the punchers, did not go across the street to the Chinaman's. They forked their ponies, and went cantering south toward their own spreads.

It did not take much noise to awaken the Celestial. The men went inside and sprawled at a table while they listened to the Chinaman in his kitchen rattle pots and pans. Soon the welcome aroma of fresh coffee reached them.

Zanders, who had been deep in thought, turned suddenly to the big S 4 rancher. "What do you figger we ought to do, Jim?" he asked. "You hankerin' to ride herd with them woolly nurses?"

"No, I ain't," the cowman retorted sourly, "but now that we're started, I reckon we've got to. Somethin's got to be done about the nestors. At the rate they're pilin' into this county, there soon won't be room enough for our stock."

"Why not take the Doc's suggestion?" the Squared X rancher demanded. "That sounded like good horse sense to me. Danged if I want to get mixed up in another range war. The last one cost me plenty."

Just then the Chinaman came through his swinging doors with plates of hot food. For a time there was no sound but the clink of knives and forks on plates and the occasional grunts of the men. The hot coffee, weak as it was, and the steaming cakes softened the tempers of all of them.

Croll was the first to push his plate back and lean back in his chair while he rolled a quirley. His glance settled on Zanders, who was still busily eating.

"Pat," he said suddenly, "you're younger 'an me. I don't know what your idea is, but it strikes me we've been kind of hard on the medico. I ain't the kind to back water, but when I'm wrong, I reckon I ain't ashamed to admit it. I was just thinkin' how I'd feel if I'd been in Jan Jungward's shoes, and I had a daughter that was sick."

Zanders' grey eyes, attentive and watchful, focused on the mustachioed rancher over the rim of his coffee cup. Croll had been the head of the county board for a good many years now, and the Squared X owner had learned to admire the old cowman's judgment.

"Cut it a little finer, Jim," he said. "I'm listenin'."

"Well, it's just this," Croll drawled. "I'm comin' to think that maybe the medico did right when he passed up the weddin' to look after that gal. 'Course I'm a mite prejudiced, for I never could see what he saw in that sheep tender's daughter. Still, I'll admit she was pretty."

Canary Flack nodded his yellow head, and chimed in with, "Prettier than a spotted dog under a red wagon."

Zanders nodded, too, but did not interrupt. He emptied his cup and pushed his chair back from the table. Then he pulled a pipe from his pocket and began to pack it carefully, his glance still on the S 4 cowman.

"Maybe it was fate," Croll went on, nodding his grey head sagely. "Whitey broke his leg that day, and Cliff set it 'fore he'd think of goin' to his weddin'. I couldn't blame him for that. And then Jungward comes in and asks him to look after his daughter. I heard the old coot pulled a gun on the medico to make him do it."

All of them heard the strike of hoofs from the street, but none of them paid any attention. Croll looked at the end of his cigarette, and then started to speak again. "What I'm drivin' at is this. We done wrong in leavin' Slats there at the S Bar 8 to hold Cliff and the sheriff. Doc's got more sense than the rest of us. He'd ought to be on our side."

Zanders' glance swiveled suddenly towards the door of the café. Slats Farwell was standing there, peering in, and anger crimsoned his blue eyes. "Next time you give me orders to watch the medico and Plum," he rasped out, "leave a couple of other waddies with me. I've been in the calaboose since midnight. They both of them piled on me and trussed me up like a fowl ready for the roastin' pan. Then they brought me here to town and threw me in the jug. Plum just let me out a minute ago."

Croll and Zanders exchanged glances. Canary's long face twisted into a snarl. "Do you reckon that's who it was that trapped us in that nestor shack?" he demanded.

"I'm guessin' it was," the S 4 puncher exploded. "That'd be just like them two jiggers. That's why you weren't plugged in the back, Pat, when you opened the door. That's why none of us was hurt. They just figured to hold us there till our tempers cooled. Come on, men! I'm thinkin' we got to have a little palaver with Dorr and the medico. Maybe a little taste of their own medicine'd help."

# CHAPTER THIRTEEN

IT WAS an angry fivesome who marched down the street to the medico's cottage and turned in the gate. Croll knocked loudly on the door and, when no one answered, tried the knob and entered.

His keen glance, sweeping the room, noted that the physician's bed had not been slept in. "Where in tarnation would he be at this time of the mornin'?" he complained.

"Out with the settlers, most likely," Zanders answered bitterly. "Stirrin' 'em up against us."

While they were standing there discussing it, they heard the crunch of boots on the gravel walk and, turning, saw Plum approaching them. All of their glances narrowed on him, and Croll growled, "Since the medico ain't here, we'll give you a piece of our tongue, Dorr. Where did you and the medico go after you threw Slats in jail?"

"I can't speak for the Doc," the ex-sheriff replied soberly, "but I figgered it was too late to stop you hotheaded fools, so I went home. Where's Cliff? Ain't he here?" He was trying hard to keep a straight face, for he noted that Zanders was scratching his side surreptitiously.

"No, he ain't here," the big S 4 rancher grumbled, "and it don't look like he's been here all night."

The news worried the ex-sheriff, and he brushed quickly by the men to see for himself. The five men watched him as he opened the closet doors, dug into bureau drawers, and searched the physician's home from top to bottom.

"It's durned queer," he remarked, when his painstaking search revealed no clues to the disappearance of the doctor. "Canary," he barked at the puncher, "run across to the stable and see if Cliff's roan is there."

And then, suddenly, a bright piece of silk caught his eye, and he stooped to pick it up from beneath the bed. He turned it over in his hand, looked at it, and finally smelled it.

"A woman's been here," he announced. "Now what gal 'ud wear a loud neckerchief like that?"

"I seen that nestor's gal wearin' one like it the last time I was in town," Zanders exclaimed. "Maybe it's hers."

Just then the big, yellow-haired puncher came back. "The medico's roan is there in the corral, Sheriff," he announced. "The younker doesn't know what time he came in. He claimed he was asleep, and didn't hear him. And Shorty don't know nothin' neither."

"He wouldn't," Slats Farwell ranted. "He was actin' as jailer."

Croll exclaimed suddenly, "You don't reckon that redheaded filly kidnapped him, do you, Dorr? Wasn't she goin' to live with Suter?"

"She didn't go there," Plum replied quickly. "Cliff rode out and left her there, but Mrs. Suter said she didn't even stop." He told them then of the physician's efforts to trail her and of his failure.

"I always figgered she was a tramp," Zanders said.

"It's a good thing the medico ain't here to hear you say that, Pat," Plum said shortly. "And I ain't agreein' with you. The Lord never made a redheaded fool. Shan Jungward's got plenty of grey matter tucked under that carrot top of hers. But why would she want to kidnap him? And did she? Somehow, it just don't make sense. I've heard of men kidnappin' gals for various reasons, but I ain't never heard of a gal doin' it to a man."

For the moment, all the men's anger against Plum and the physician was forgotten in this new mystery. They were all cudgeling their brains for a solution to the medico's disappearance. Plum's old eyes were riveted to the doctor's shelves, where he kept his bottles of pills and medicines. He was thinking that, if Cliff had been kidnapped, he would have left some clue behind him. Plum had a great deal of respect for the physician's cunning. But the room seemed bare of anything that would give him a clue.

"Slats," the old sheriff said suddenly. "You and Canary walk down the street and inquire of the folks that are awake if they've seen the doc. Maybe he's right here in town."

The two punchers followed orders, and Plum turned his attention more carefully to the shelves, while the two cowmen stood and watched him. Then, suddenly, the lawman's exclamation brought them to his side.

"He was kidnapped," Plum cried. "Sure as shootin', and by that filly. I figured he'd leave some word as to what happened to him. Look here, Jim." He pointed to a shelf where a row of bottles stood. "See that first bottle? The label says kaolin. The second is iodine, and the third is demulcent or somethin'. That spells kid. Now look at the rest of 'em. The first letters of the names on them bottles spells kidnapped. And look over there at the end. Here's four more bottles." He read the inscriptions: "Sulphate for S, hydroxide for H, ammonia for A, and nitrates for N. That spells Shan."

"Well, I'll be jiggered!" Zanders exclaimed. "A right smart trick."

"I told you the medico was the smartest hombre that ever came to this county," Plum rapped out. "Now all we've got to do is find the gal."

"What do you mean—we?" Croll growled. "The gal can have the meddlin' fool, and welcome. After what he did to us tonight, I don't give a tinker's damn what happens to the jigger. Come on, Pat. Me, I'm plenty satisfied. Let Dorr search for him if he wants to. I ain't goin' to waste none of my time doin' it."

The two men stamped out, and Plum, standing before the shelves, heard the strike of their ponies as they gathered the two punchers and went loping out of town.

"The danged bullheaded centipedes," the old lawman ranted. "If they had any sense in their heads, they'd know why Shan wanted the medico out of the way. He's the only man in the county smart enough to stop a range war. And I'm bettin' that redheaded filly is leadin' the pack of wolves that tried to burn Jeffries' spread. She's got an axe to grind. It was her dad that was killed."

Taking a last look around, the ex-sheriff closed the door and went out. He quartered across the street to his old office and sat down heavily in the swivel chair. Here he had learned to do his thinking. He was trying to hazard some guess as to where the girl and her followers would take the medico. But he was unsuccessful and, after almost an hour of this ruminating, he finally mounted his sorrel, circled the physician's cottage, and struck off towards the Springs at a slow canter.

There had been hoof marks behind the physician's home, and it was these he was following. They led him directly towards the break in the precipitous wall, of sandstone and then were lost, for the crumbling shale and stone underfoot left no trail for even a good lawman to follow.

Still he pressed on until he had reached the desert's edge. The plain was a vast area of saffron-hued and cactus-studded aridity. The gashing slopes and brakes of Hell's Acres were but a mere speck on the distant horizon; beyond them towered the rugged, saw-toothed crests of the wind-swept Dragoons, their peaks gleaming white in the miracle of the early-morning sun.

Acting on a sudden hunch, for there was no sign here to cut, Plum traversed the level wasteland for a mile or more, his keen eyes ever on the ground. Again and again his glance would lift to the horizon, and he would shake his head.

The better part of the morning had passed before he retraced his steps, and returned via the narrow pass that cut through the upthrusting, grotesque rocks that backed the Springs. And the sun had already reached its zenith when he cantered back into town.

His keen eyes noted instantly that no settlers nor settlers' wives strolled beneath the wooden awnings; moved by a sudden inspiration, he left his mount in front of the Mercantile and walked into the cool interior to greet Hank Rogers.

"How's the bunnies doin', Plum?" the store owner asked.

" 'Tain't rabbits that I got on my mind," the old lawman answered irritably. "It's the medico."

"What's he done?" Rogers demanded. He was a smooth-faced, smallish man, with a touch of grey at his temples, and with close-set, shrewd eyes.

" 'Tain't what he's done, it's where he's gone. That nestor gal kidnapped him last night."

If the old lawman had dropped a bombshell in the store, it wouldn't have caused so much consternation. The store owner's mouth sagged wide, and his eyes bulged out until they looked as if they might pop right out of his round face.

"Kidnapped!" he ejaculated. "Kidnapped!"

Anxious to unburden himself, the old lawman told him of the bottles and of his attempt at trailing. "It would happen when Bonnett's out of town," he complained. "And the cowmen won't lift a hand to help me. They're all sore at Cliff. The thing has got me buffaloed. I ain't got any idea even where to look for him."

"Have you been out north of the Springs?" Rogers asked. "Seen any of the settlers?"

"That's what I was goin' to ask you."

"There ain't been a single one in town today," the store owner answered. "Fact is, I ain't had a darned customer today."

Plum left the Mercantile and started across the street, intending to head for the Chinaman's. He did not feel like cooking a meal for himself. But halfway across he stopped dead and stared at the Mansion House. The sign that, until yesterday, had hung on the locked door, was gone, and, for the first time, he noticed that the old rocking chairs were again on the walk. Grinning like a Cheshire cat, he retraced his steps and marched straight for the hotel's entrance.

But he did not enter. Instead, he cat-footed to the window and surreptitiously peeked through the glass, his glance studying the darker interior. Satisfied with what he saw, he hurried back across the street, lifted himself to the sorrel's back and went flying out of town.

Reaching his little ranch, he ground-hitched his pony and entered the barn. For the better part of half an hour he remained there; when he came out, he had six fat frying rabbits skinned and cleaned and wrapped in newspapers. Again he swung to the saddle and headed the sorrel toward town.

Just a little apprehensively, he hitched the pony to the Mansion House rail and, with the package under his arm, strolled nonchalantly inside. Maw Blane was behind the counter, in exactly the same place as when he had peeked through the window.

Her glance lifted from the paper she had been reading, and she scowled blackly. "Merciful Heavens!" she exclaimed. "You're worse than a bad penny. What do you want?"

The old lawman was so completely taken aback by the reception he could not answer. He could only stand there, open-mouthed, staring at her.

"Well?" she snapped, as the silence lengthened. And then suddenly the black look left her face, and her lips crescented into a smile. "Why weren't you here to meet me when the stage rolled in? Lookin' after those pesky critters of yours, I suppose. What's the matter with you? Have you lost your tongue?"

Plum gulped a couple of times and then, with a sudden yelp of gladness, dropped the package to the floor and went running around in back of the counter. Before Maw could offer the slightest resistance, he had folded her into his arms and was giving her a bear hug.

She tried to struggle free, but Plum's arms were hard and tough and, without waiting for her permission, he gave her a resounding smack on the lips. Not until then did he release her.

"Durned if you ain't a sight for sore eyes," he cried. "Gawd Awmighty! I'm tickled to see you."

"Act your age," she snapped back at him, but her face was red, and there was a soft light in her eyes. "Where did you learn to kiss like that? Been cuttin' capers while I was out of town?"

"Not as many as I've been hearin' about you," he derided. "I heard how you acted in El Paso. Maw, you'd ought to be ashamed of yourself. 'Tain't no way for an engaged woman to act."

"Engaged to who?" she snorted. "Not to you, by cricky. When I pick me a new husband, I'll get a younger and handsomer man. What have you got in that package?"

He walked over to it and picked it up. "Well," he drawled, grinning, "if you ain't my fiancée, I reckon this isn't for you. *Adios,* you old battle-axe."

Maw Blane came from behind the counter like a charging ram. She was not a big woman, but she was broad of hip, big-bosomed, and strong as an ox. "Battle-axe, is it?" she screamed. "I'll teach an old moth-eaten coot like you to call me names."

Plum met her halfway and stopped her headlong flight, wrapping his arms about her and holding her tight. "You're the prettiest woman in the whole state," he wheedled. "Honest, Maw! I'm loco about you. That there was a—term of endearment. And you are my fiancée, ain't you?"

"Well!" Unable to move her arms, she looked up at him. The fire died from her eyes, and suddenly she put her grey head on his shoulder and began to cry. "If you're proposin' to me, Dorr Plum," she said at last, her voice muffled by his shoulder, "it's about time. What in God's name did you think I came back here for?"

Plum forgot all his troubles in the ecstasy of that moment.

She pulled away from him finally, and stood with her hands on her hips, her glance searching his face. She said, "I've always known you were loco, Dorr. Now suppose you pick up that package and give it to me."

Grinning, he stooped and picked it up. He felt a little ashamed now of his present, and he cursed himself for not having bought something from the Mercantile.

"It's just a mess of rabbits I was honin' to have you cook for me, Maw," he said sheepishly. "I didn't have time to get nothin' else. I didn't know you were comin' today." And then the memory of the physician's disappearance pricked him, and he added, "The medico was kidnapped last night by that nestor gal. I've been out tryin' to trail 'em since sunup. And there's another war a-startin'. Hell's goin' to bust loose on this range again."

This woman knew how to treat men with worries. She took the old lawman out into the kitchen with her while she prepared the rabbits and his lunch. She listened attentively to his recital of events from the time she had left with Nancy Starweather until her return. She let him talk, interrupting only occasionally to clear up some point in his recital that she did not clearly understand. Not until he was fed and had pushed back his chair did she tell him what she thought.

"It's clear, Dorr," she said. "Nancy had a right to be mad about the medico goin' to that girl. But that's over and done with now. I ain't blamin' him. He was only doin' his duty as a physician. And that Shan Jungward's smart. Smarter than most of the men in these parts. You're the only one that seems to have kept a level head on his shoulders. Now suppose you leave me to figure things out from the gal's angle. There's no need to worry about the doc. He's well able to take care of himself, and if she's loco about him, as you say, there won't no harm come to him."

Relieved by her talk, and feeling much better now that his stomach was filled with food, the old lawman finally forked his sorrel and headed for home. He turned the pony loose to graze, fed his rabbits, and then took a dozen of them into the barn to skin and dress, for Maw had signified her intention of serving fried rabbit for the evening's meal at the Mansion House.

His sleeves were rolled up, and the carcasses of the rabbits on the butchering table, when he was suddenly aware of someone standing close to him, and turned quickly. Shan Jungward stood there with a long-barreled Colt in her fist, the muzzle of it pointing at Plum.

Surprise and bewilderment twisted the lawman's face, and he cried, "Where in tarnation did you drop from?"

"Out of the sky, Mr. Plum," she said quickly, and smiled. "Unbuckle your gunbelt and let it drop. You're comin' with me."

"Like hell I am," the old lawman gritted, and made whirling motion, his hands streaking for his guns.

A single shot blasted the stillness of the barn. Plum's hands remained where they had dropped, locked to the butts of his twin Colts. One of those weapons was useless, he knew. The slug from Shan's gun had cut through the holster and smashed the cylinder. The old lawman could tell that by the numbness of his right arm.

# CHAPTER FOURTEEN

THERE was a long period of silence as the glances of the lawman and the girl met and held. In all his years of sheriffing, Plum had never before faced a woman with a gun, certainly not a beautiful one. His natural instincts were to whip the other weapon out and at least have a try with it, but his common sense told him that to do so would only be running a needless risk. Shan Jungward had already demonstrated that she could shoot—and straight. It would cost him a pretty penny to have that one favorite weapon of his repaired.

Shan sensed the conflict that raged in the ex-sheriff's breast. "I'm not honin' to hurt you, Mr. Plum," she said softly, "but I can't guarantee that my next shot'll be as accurate. You'd better take your hands off the butts of them guns and unbuckle your belt. Besides," she added, and a warm smile crescented her long, curving lips, "I don't think you'd shoot a woman."

Plum grudgingly removed his fingers from the weapons and moved them to his belt buckle, but his glance did not leave her face. He was seeing something in this girl that he had never noticed before. She was not only decidedly pretty, but a woman with plenty of courage. Even when he had reached for his weapons, with a speed that had frightened case-hardened outlaws, she had not wavered nor shown fear. And she stood facing him now with complete confidence in the outcome.

"Danged if you ain't got more sand than the Painted Desert," he grumbled. "But what in tarnation's the idea of bargin' in here and ruinin' one of my guns? I ain't the law in this county no more. I'm a rabbit rancher."

"I know all that," she answered sweetly, "but I realize too that, with Bonnett away, the folks of this county'll naturally turn to you to help 'em. That's what I'm tryin' to guard against. We're goin' to see that the law is missin' when we get ready to strike."

"And that's why you kidnapped the doc?"

Surprise widened her eyes. "How did you know that?" she asked.

As he unbuckled his guns and let them slide over his hips to the dirt floor, he told her of the medico's rearrangement of the bottles. "You'll have to get up mighty early in the mornin' to slip anythin' over on that medico," he finished with a faint smile.

"Does anyone else know that I've got him a prisoner?" she demanded.

"I reckon the whole county knows it by this time. But you don't need to worry about that. Croll and Zanders, and I callate the sheepmen too, figure it's good riddance. Cliff ain't got many friends since he nursed you back to health. You'd ought to be ashamed of yourself for treatin' him thataway after what he done for you. Saved your life, didn't he?"

She flushed under his steady gaze. "I ain't forgotten that," she shrugged. Then she added, a little waspishly, "You don't need to worry about Cliff's health. We're not goin' to harm him, and I think you'd better march outside now. I've wasted enough time already, and we've got a long ways to go 'fore sundown."

"What about my rabbits, ma'am?" he demanded, as he suddenly remembered his warrens. "If you're goin' to hold me prisoner for a spell, the critters'll die."

"You don't have to worry about that, neither," she answered quickly. "When we get where we're goin', you can furnish me with orders. I'll see that all your bunnies are taken care of."

She stepped away from him as he moved toward the door. In the opening, he stopped and looked back at her. "I just fixed a dozen of the critters for Maw to serve for supper tonight. They won't be no good 'less they're kept in the cooler. What about them?"

"Stop your arguin'," she snapped. "I'll see that they're delivered in time."

He moved outside. Two riders, their faces hidden by black masks, sat their ponies there, waiting. One of them had already saddled and bridled the old lawman's sorrel, and, with a grunt, Plum lifted himself to the saddle. Instantly a rope dropped over his bony shoulders and was drawn tight. Shan whipped the neckerchief from her neck and handed it to the man nearest. He kneed his pony close to the sorrel and tied the silk securely over Plum's eyes.

"This is a danged uncomfortable way to ride," the lawman complained. "I ain't got no idea of makin' a break with the three of you watchin' me."

"Maybe not," Shan answered crisply, "but we ain't goin' to take no chances. An' the less you know about where we're takin' you, the better off we'll be."

The cavalcade started off, but the old lawman, smart from his years of trailing criminals, knew instantly that the two men had gone, and that it was Shan alone who was guarding him. He knew, too, that the rope that lashed his arms to his sides stretched to the girl's saddle, for he could feel the occasional tug of it, as the two ponies loped across the mesa.

He tried to hazard a guess at the direction they were taking from the slope of the ground and the sound of the sorrel's hoofs, but after almost an hour of steady riding he was completely at sea. At first he had thought they were heading for the Springs; for a time he had felt the sun on his face. But then, suddenly, it had changed to his back. A sudden cool wind befuddled him further, and the changing tempo of his pony's hoofs. The sorrel slowed and began to walk. Plum could hear shale crunching underfoot, then solid rock, then shale again, and finally grass. Someone spoke to his captor, and the old lawman's pony came to an abrupt halt.

Ears cocked and straining to hear, Plum could distinguish nothing in the whispered conversation that went on somewhere nearby. A little surreptitiously, he tried to move his hands up to his face to slip the blindfold down. Instantly the rope tightened and the girl's voice rapped out at him:

"I wouldn't try that, Mr. Plum. It's only a short ways now."

A second later the ex-sheriff heard the creak of saddle leather, and then the fading beat of hoofs. The sorrel again started moving. After what seemed at least another full hour of riding, the horses stopped abruptly. The rope about his arms was loosened, and strong hands lifted him from the saddle. He tried to struggle free, but he was no match for the man who held him, and again the girl's voice called out:

"You might just as well take it easy, Mr. Plum. If you keep that up, I'll have to have your hands tied back of you."

"Dammit!" he exploded wrathfully. "You ain't heard the last of this yet, Shan Jungward. I'll have the law on you. Kidnappin' is a mighty serious offense in this county."

The girl's silvery laugh was like the tinkling of bells. She said, "Take him inside, Harry. I'm sure the doc'll be glad to see him."

The same strong hands pushed him ahead. There was grass underfoot now, and then solid rock. Suddenly the blindfold was removed from his face, and he blinked to get his eyes accustomed to the light. His glance swiveled quickly around the room they had brought him to, and he saw Cliff.

"Danged if this don't beat all," he growled.

"Welcome to your new home," the physician responded with a wide grin. "You might as well make the best of it, Dorr. They feed their prisoners well, and there are good beds to sleep on. We've no longer got a hand in this game. Shan's got the deck stacked, and she's holding all the aces."

Plum sat down a little wearily in a chair. This was a cave of some sort he was in, but it was high-ceilinged and roomy. The sandstone walls were dry, and there seemed to be plenty of fresh air. A small fire was burning against the far wall, and the smoke spiraled steadily upwards. There were three iron cots against the opposite wall; four chairs, one of them an old rocker, and a crude table had been planted in the middle of the room. A coal oil lamp burned on the table.

The two settlers who had brought him in had retired, leaving the two old friends alone. Plum's glance, having finished its swift inventory, returned to study the face of the physician.

"Doggoned if you don't seem well pleased with your surroundin's," he remarked.

"Not exactly pleased," Cliff nodded, "but more or less contented. Shan brought a good many of my medical books for me to read. I've been brushing up on some of them. How would you like to have a look around outside?"

"Will they let us out of here?"

"Certainly," the physician responded with a grin. "That business of keeping you blindfolded is just Shan's flare for the dramatic."

Plum followed the medico through a heavy door that had been crudely hewn from logs. He found himself in a narrow valley, perhaps a hundred yards in width and close to a mile in length. Cows were grazing contentedly on the lush grass, hogs were rooting in the soil, and, at the far end, the old lawman saw a small flock of sheep. A rooster crowed, the noise echoing from the sheer sandstone cliffs that hemmed this tiny valley in on all sides.

Along the base of the precipitous walls were many caves similar to the one out of which Plum had just come. He could see settlers' wives working in front of these, some of them washing, others doing household chores. Children played in the small stand of pine that flanked the base of the cliff on the opposite side.

"Where in the devil are we?" the old lawman exclaimed, his eyes popping out. "There ain't nothin' about this spot that even looks familiar. It ain't any part of Hell's Acres."

"No! You're right there," the physician answered, "and your guess is as good as mine. I suppose it took you about two hours to get here. It did me, for I timed it carefully. Now, where could you ride in that length of time and find a spot like this?"

"You couldn't, durn it. The whole business don't make sense. How long do you figger they'll hold us here?"

"Again your guess is as good as mine, Dorr. I rather like it, myself. It just happens that there aren't any serious illnesses that require my attention in the county. I've needed a vacation for a long time, and I'm getting one. Shan sets almost as good a table as Maw does."

"She came back today," Plum growled, suddenly remembering. "Just as cantankerous as ever, but still the same old Maw. And this is goin' to worry her plenty."

Cliff put his arm across the lawman's shoulder affectionately. "Buck up, old timer," he chided. "You've waited a long time to propose to her. Another week or two won't cut any ice."

"I done it today," Plum answered sheepishly.

"Why, you old mossyhorn!" The medico laughed. "Congratulations!"

"Congratulations be damned!" Plum snapped irritably. "How do I know that redheaded hellion'll ever let me out of here? Maybe Maw'll think I got scared and ran out on her."

They heard the strike of hoofs, and both men turned their attention toward the end of the valley, where they saw five riders heave into view around an upthrusting pinnacle of rock. They came at a swift pace down the valley, with the girl leading them. At the entrance to a cave not more than fifty feet from where the two men were standing, they brought their ponies to a halt. All of them dismounted, and the two men watching saw the riders remove saddles and bridles and turn the ponies loose. Shan talked for a minute with the big, rawboned Harry Suter, then turned in the direction of the medico and the ex-sheriff.

"I took your rabbits to Mrs. Blane," she announced, "and you don't need to worry none about your spread. One of the men just come from there. They have all been fed and taken care of for the night."

"You saw Maw?" Plum exclaimed.

Shan shook her head and laughed. "No, I made sure not to be seen, but the rabbits is in the cooler, and I left a note for her, tellin' her that you had been called away on important business."

"Durned if you ain't got more gall!" the old lawman exclaimed angrily.

"You see, Dorr," Cliff remarked, grinning, "I told you that there was nothing to worry about. Shan seems to be able to figure out everything. I wouldn't be a mite surprised but what she'd be taking my place at some sickbed, if the need arose."

There was more talk, and then the girl left abruptly. Nor did Plum and the physician have a chance to speak to her again for the next three days. Things were going on in this hidden valley that the two friends could only guess at. Gaunt-faced settlers stood guard in front of the cave and refused to allow them to leave it for more than a few minutes at a time.

The swift drumming of hoofs was an almost hourly occurrence. These two men locked inside knew that the gods of war were hovering over Painted Springs and Brant County. They had been able to gather that much from the few words they had overheard. Shan was leading the settlers in a fight that threatened to exterminate one faction or the oher, and so far she had apparently gotten the better of it.

On the morning of the third day, the girl entered the abode of the two men and confronted them. Her eyes were deeply shadowed, and it was instantly apparent to the medico that Shan Jungward was riding solely on her nerves.

"Would you mind steppin' outside, Mr. Plum?" she asked. "I'd like to talk to Cliff alone."

The lawman started to object, but a glance from the physician made him change his mind. Grumbling a little, he complied.

"I've got bad news for you, Cliff," Shan announced in a tired voice when the door had closed on the sheriff's back. "Poke Bonnett had disappeared."

The physician was startled, and he was more puzzled when the girl explained. Bonnett had never reached Yuma with his prisoner. Two men had hailed the stage just beyond Hell's Acres and begged for a lift. The driver, seeing that they were unarmed and finding their explanations plausible, had allowed them to climb into the vehicle. They had reached Coyote Wells that night. Here a new driver had taken charge, and the mustanger who drove the Concord between Painted Springs and the Wells had promptly forgotten Bonnett and his prisoner, whom he had seen re-enter the vehicle and go on towards the next stage stop.

At Dry Lake, the other driver had seen the men with Bonnett and the prisoner mount horses left for them and head toward

Tombstone, apparently trying to save time by using ponies instead of the stage for that part of the journey. But none of the four men had appeared in Tombstone. Word had just been brought to Painted Springs that the sheriff of that county, investigating another matter, had come upon the body of a man identified as the prisoner, and the body of another who was identified as one of the men who had hailed the stage near Hell's Acres. "Shotgun" Rand, the driver of the stage between Painted Springs and Coyote Wells, had, at the request of the authorities, gone on to Tombstone to look at the corpses.

"I don't see any reason for you to be downhearted over the news," the physician remarked, and his grey eyes were hard and bitter. "It's as good as what you planned. You wanted all three of us locked up here so that you could have a free hand to bring the ranchers to their knees."

"I did, Cliff," Shan answered, "but I meant none of you any harm. I liked Poke. He was one of the few men who was decent to me, and he was *your* friend. Can't you realize what that means to me?"

Cliff put his hands on the girl's shoulders and looked down at her. "I've told you many times, Shan," he said softly, "that love is a funny thing. It just doesn't make sense. I admire you for your courage and your beauty—I can't help that—but I don't love you and I never will."

She pulled away from him, and all the softness that had shone in her eyes was gone now, leaving them bleak and angry. "That settles it," she rapped out savagely.

"Settles what?" he asked, lips tightening.

She laughed, and her laughter was bitter, mocking, filled with venom. "I'm goin' to tear down all that you have built up, Dr. Cliff Monroe. You won't be there to see it, but I'm goin' to make this county pay dearly for the killin' of my father and the disappearance of my mother and brother. Tonight we'll start our raidin'. And we won't stop with the cattle and the sheep. It will be humans this time. I've got a score to settle." With a choking cry, she turned and fled.

# CHAPTER FIFTEEN

PLUM came back when the girl ran through the door, and the physician, tight-lipped, told him what had just occurred. "It's another range war that will make the last one look like a strawberry festival," he announced. "Unless we can find some way to stop her."

"If we was outside," the old lawman gritted, "we wouldn't have no trouble, but after what she just told you, I reckon they'd put a slug through our briskets if they caught us tryin' to escape. I knowed that gal was goin' to cause trouble in this county. I've had a feelin' in my bones about her. These settlers follow her like a lot of sheep. She's got the power to stir 'em up. I reckon they've already tasted rancher blood, and liked it."

The physician mulled that over in his mind while pacing back and forth, and then suddenly stopped as he remembered Maida Suter's greeting to him the day he had brought Shan to her homestead. The woman had been far from friendly toward the girl. She had seemed pleased at the knowledge that Shan Jungward was not coming to live with them. And if Maida Suter disliked the girl, undoubtedly there were others who felt the same. Shan had the power to stir men, but it was an ability that the women could not appreciate.

"If we could get to the settlers' wives," Cliff suggested, "it might be a way of stopping her."

"But how?"

Cliff pointed out to him the animosity of the womenfolks toward Shan. "I don't imagine any of them took kindly to this idea of leaving their homes at the mercy of the ranchers. Now here's an idea. I've got one patient here who is of the perpetually ailing type. If I send her word that I'd like to see her, she will immediately think that something is wrong with her, and she'll come willingly. Through her we may reach the others and sound them out."

Plum did not have much faith in the idea, but he followed the physician's advice, called to one of the guards and asked him to give the medico's message to Mrs. Huseman.

The woman came finally, and entered the cave where Cliff sat reading. Plum made himself inconspicuous in a corner, while he listened to Cliff telling the settler's wife what he had finally decided was wrong with her. From this he veered around adroitly until he was sounding her out with skillful questions.

She was a smallish woman, with faded blonde hair streaked with grey, and with a perpetually sallow complexion. And when the physician told her that a cave was no place for her to live in her frail condition, and that the fresh air of the mesa was ideal, she demanded bitterly, "But what can I do, Doctor? What can any of us do? We have to live here while our menfolks follow that red-haired—" She stopped suddenly, realizing that she had been about to say something against the girl who was trying to help them. She did not want to show disloyalty to the cause.

"Shan is a fine young woman, Mrs. Huseman," the medico exclaimed quickly, "but, I'm afraid, a misguided one. All of this is so unnecessary. There is no need for you people to hide here in this tiny valley. which isn't big enough to support one family. And what is happening to your homes? The places that you have worked so hard to homestead? The ranchers are not so bad as they are painted. I know them, Mrs. Huseman. I had convinced them that the right thing to do was to sit down with the settlers and decide things peacefully. They would have done that if your men hadn't killed Mullaby's sheep and tried to burn Jeffries' house."

There was more argument in the same vein. Plum grinned admiringly as the physician piled fact on fact, and slowly but surely convinced this faded, work-worn woman that Shan's plan was suicide.

Mrs. Huseman was more than ready to believe. She had felt undeniably better since she had been taking the medico's pills. And, like Mrs. Suter, in her heart she had no love for the bright-haired girl who led the settlers.

Within an hour, Mrs. Suter called. Her husband was the leader beneath Shan, and she had seen him looking at the young and pretty girl with more than just admiration in his eyes. Jealousy had flamed in her breast. The physician had no difficulty in convincing her that the settlers' wives were fools to remain hidden in this canyon while their menfolks plundered and burned on the outside.

When she had gone, Cliff grinned at the old lawman. "I think we're going to clip the wings of Miss Shan Jungward," he said. "It's too bad. I like and admire her, but she's put herself outside and above the law. Not even a pretty woman can do that, Dorr. Shan's riding for a fall, and it looks like you and I have been picked to give it to her."

"It won't make me feel bad," Plum growled.

Noon came, and one of the settlers' wives brought in the prisoners' lunch. She stopped for a moment's chat, and both men noticed that she appeared grimly resolved about something.

Allowed to sit outside and smoke, Plum and the medico moved a couple of chairs and sat there contentedly watching the sun's shadows lengthen.

"I ain't figured just where this spot is yet," the lawman remarked, as he rolled himself a smoke, "but I got a durn good hunch. If you'll notice the rock hereabouts, you'll see that it's the same formation and texture as the sandstone in back of the Springs. I callate this little valley is just about in the center."

"If the womenfolks don't disappoint us," Cliff answered, "we'll soon know."

A group of riders appeared suddenly at the end of the valley. Both men's glances narrowed on them, and Cliff sighed, "Somebody's hurt."

Shan was not with the four men, who came on until they reached the medico. Three of them helped the fourth man from the saddle. Crimson dyed his shoulder, and his face was twisted with pain. It was Ruddy Huseman.

The medico stretched the settler out on the table inside and adjusted the lamp to throw its light on the wound. The others grouped around, curiosity widening their eyes. Plum cut the man's shirt from the upper part of his body, while the physician opened his kit. Cliff did not ask any questions, but immediately started to work. The man grunted and locked his teeth against the pain of the scalpel. Cliff had just removed the slug, which was imbedded deep in the muscle and lodged against the bone, when the settler's wife came running in.

"It isn't serious, Mrs. Huseman," the physician said reassuringly. "Just a slight shoulder wound. No need for him to be quiet longer than a day or two."

"Thank God!" the woman exclaimed, twisting her hands together, and with tears silvering her lids.

Cliff cleaned and bandaged the wound. The three settlers helped Huseman to his feet, and, with one on each side to steady him, marched him outside and down the valley to the man's cave home.

A few minutes later, Cliff and Plum heard swiftly fading hoofbeats and knew that the men had gone. The ex-sheriff looked at the physician, shaking his head knowingly.

"There'll be more like that, and worse, if we don't get out of here," the medico said with a shrug. "But I think it helped. It will bring home to these women what they have to face."

Once again the two men sat in the chairs. Neither of them said anything. Their two guards were close. Twilight darkened the valley, bringing the first cool touch of a faint breeze that whirled down from the tops of the precipitous cliffs that surrounded them.

A woman came to the entrance of her cave, peered up and down the valley, and then, with sudden determination, approached one of the guards. The ex-sheriff and the medico, watching her, saw her stop in front of her husband and face him. Her words reached the two prisoners distinctly.

"I'm not going to stay in this terrible canyon another night," she announced in a bitter voice. "I'm taking my children, and I'm going home."

"But you can't do that, Ma," the man answered.

She put her hands on her hips, planted her feet firmly, and retorted angrily, "And who's to stop me? Not that redheaded hussy, I'll wager! And you're going with me, Sam Bellew. I've had enough of this foolishness."

Her voice reached down the valley and could be heard by every man, woman, and child in the canyon. They came running out. Another woman, gathering courage from this one, came hurrying up to face the settler who stood guard. Her voice lifted in much the same vein.

Mrs. Suter came marching out. "We're all leaving," she announced triumphantly. "Pack your things. If my husband hasn't sense enough to know which side his bread is buttered on, he can go to the devil."

Plum grinned at the physician. "I guess you pulled a Royal Flush out of that stacked deck, Cliff," he remarked. "It looks like we're goin' to sleep in our own beds this night."

"There will be no sleep tonight for either of us," the medico answered gruffly. "We've got to stop Shan before it's too late."

Mrs. Suter, finished with her announcement, came up to the two prisoners. "You two can gather your things together," she said. "We're all leaving this horrible place."

Later, the two men watched the preparations. The cows were rounded up, and the hogs gathered. These were started out of the valley first, with three of the settlers herding them along. Horses were saddled, and belongings lashed to the cantles. Women lifted themselves to the animals' backs and took children in their arms.

Mrs. Suter again approached the two men. "You two will have to ride double on the sheriff's horse," she announced. "We haven't enough ponies for all. My husband's not here, and he might need this place to hide in. You'll both go out blindfolded and roped, the same way you came in."

Plum grumbled at that, but the physician nodded his head in agreement. The ex-sheriff found his sorrel, roped and saddled him. Mrs. Suter took neckerchiefs and blindfolded them both, then helped first the old lawman, and then the medico to the animal's back. She found a length of rope and securely lashed the sheriff's hands to the horn, and the medico's in back of him. In that way the sorrel was led down the valley until he had joined the rest of the procession.

It was almost dark now. Around the two men women and horses crowded. They could hear the bleating of sheep, the steady strike of hoofs, the grunts of the hogs. Then, once again, the tempo of the noises changed as the procession moved steadily ahead over shale, then rock, and then shale again.

The sorrel suddenly broke into a canter, and both men had to cling tight with their knees to keep from being bounced off. In this way they crossed what seemed like miles of prairie, until they were both as befuddled as ever as to their direction.

"Where in tarnation is that danged female takin' us?" Plum growled.

"You'll find out in good time," the physician answered.

Then, suddenly, the procession stopped. Someone untied their hands and told them to remove their bandages. It was pitch black now, but both men knew instantly that they were in front of Suter's cabin, for Mrs. Suter stood looking up at them, and the dark outlines of the homestead and outbuildings were visible in the background.

"You can go on to your homes now," she announced. And then she put her hand on the medico's arm and said pleadingly, "You said you could stop this trouble. We're all depending on you, Doctor. And you, too, Dorr Plum. God knows what will happen to us all out here on the prairie. If you should see my man, send him home."

"We'll do all that we can," the physician promised.

They left her standing there, and headed the sorrel for town. Riding double, and both silent, they reached the main street of Painted Springs, where light striped the dusty thoroughfare, revealing the furtive movements of waiting men. They saw the brands of Squared X ponies, also S 4 and Crossed S markings. Further down the street other ponies drowsed at the hitching rails—animals branded Bar 20 and S Bar 8.

Suddenly, as the light from the saloon cut across their faces, a yell went up, and men came crowding around them, demanding to know where they had been. Jim Croll was there; Pat Zanders; Henry Scoles, the horse breeder; and a sprinkling of sheepmen.

Cliff slid from the sorrel's back and, with the ex-sheriff at his heels, filed into the Lone Deuce. Roney's eyes widened, and then grinned a welcome. He slid a new bottle and clean glasses down the bar to them.

"Drink up, you jiggers," he cried. "You're sure both a sight for sore eyes. Where in hell you been?"

Plum turned his glance on the medico and winked. "A right curious crowd, ain't they, Cliff?" he remarked. "Maybe you'd better tell 'em. My gullet's too durned dry for any long speeches. Besides which, I got to make a personal call at the Mansion House."

The medico finished his drink and then turned to Jim Croll, who had once been his friend, and who was the head of the county board. The old rancher's face was definitely pinched by lack of sleep and worry. All the rest of these men's faces were sober, too, and all of their belts gun-hung, studded with fresh cartridges.

Speaking steadily, Cliff told them of his kidnapping, of the hidden lair of the nestors, and finally of how he had convinced the settlers' wives that Shan Jungward's plan was suicide. "I've promised them," he said, "that the ranchers would meet with them here in town. Are you men going to make that promise come true?"

"What about the gal?" a sheepman demanded. "You aimin' to let her go free, after what she's done?"

The physician shook his head. "Shan Jungward has put herself above the law, men," he said. "Dorr and I don't know what has happened these last few days, but whatever she's responsible for she will have to answer for in court."

"The pack of coyotes has done plenty," Zanders gritted. "They've burned all my haystacks and set fire to my barn. Mullaby's nursin' a bullet in the leg, and we've already buried one of the sheepherders. They've cut fences and scattered our stock all over the county. We'd planned to give 'em a taste of their own medicine tonight. When we get finished, there ain't goin' to be a shack nor a fence standin' north of the Springs, and if there's any of the squareheads runnin' loose on the prairie, we aim to treat them like their menfolks have treated our women. We're finished with loco ideas of meetin's, Doc. We're declarin' war. Either they move out, load up women, dogs and chickens, or—"

The cowman did not finish, but the tone of his voice was threat enough. Zanders had always been a God-fearing, respected member of the community. The loss he had suffered at the hands of the hoemen had changed that. He had seen his hay burned, hay that would have carried his stock through the long winter. He had seen his wife and his children frightened by the raiding settlers, and his barn go up in flames. He had been pushed to the limit.

Cliff, watching these men who backed up the rancher, knew that nothing short of a miracle could hold them back now. To a man, they felt as Zanders did. Their tempers had reached the breaking point. There were only three men in the town that the physician could depend on for help: Roney, Plum, and possibly Hank Rogers, who derived most of his business from the settlers.

# CHAPTER SIXTEEN

THE medico had to think fast. He had given his promise to the settlers, and now, in some way, he had to make good. Four men were leading this crew of revengeful ranchers: Pat Zanders, Jim Croll, Clem Jeffries and Mullaby. With those four out of the way, the others would do nothing.

Neither Cliff nor the old sheriff had guns, and argument was of no avail, for Plum, anxious to add a word for peace, had tried to reason with them, and the men would not even listen to him.

Zanders was facing the physician, with his guns hanging within easy reach. Jim Croll was close beside him. Mullaby flanked them both. In back of them crowded their punchers, their herders, and the gunnies hired for the occasion. The only one missing was Jeffries.

The medico made his decision swiftly. Without turning, he set his glass on the bar, and then, without warning, drove his knotted fist for the point of Zanders' jaw. The rancher's body arched backward, throwing Mullaby off balance, and catapulting him into the men who crowded in back of him.

Quick to take his cue, Plum reached for Croll and locked both arms around the big rancher's waist, pinning his arms tight to his sides. The physician snatched Zanders' gun from its holster and leveled it on the three ranchers, whose hands now were dipping for guns.

"Claw the sky, all of you," the medico bellowed. "I'm the ramrod of Painted Springs now, and I'll drill the first man that makes a move for his guns. There isn't going to be any raid on the settlers tonight. I'm attending to that. Snake the guns of all of them," he ordered Plum.

The old lawman already had Croll's twin weapons; he shoved one into his waistband, and helped the physician menace the crowd with the other. And then another ally helped them from the rear. Tim Roney, his blue eyes like agates, reared up from behind the scarred mahogany of his bar with a scatter-gun in his fists.

"Lift, you hotheaded fools!" he grated. "I'm backin' the medico to the last play."

"You'll pay for this," Croll growled through clenched teeth. "What you aimin' to do?"

"I'll gut-shoot you, Doc," Zanders threatened, rubbing his jaw. "No damned medico can do that to me."

Cliff's keen glance, sweeping the ugly faces of these men, saw the head of one turn, saw him make a sudden break for the door. It was one of Mullaby's hired gunhawks. The physician's gun muzzle followed him and barked once, just as the man made a swift dive for the safety of the night. The gunhawk crumpled there with a slug through his leg.

"Now, if there's any more of you fools want to try a getaway," the medico rapped out, "I'll do the same to you. Lift your hands high, and line up against the wall."

Roney kicked a box close to him, climbed on that and from there to the top of his bar, where his scatter-gun would be more effective.

Sullenly, caught flat-footed by Cliff's swift action, the men pushed back against the wall. Gun in hand, Plum moved by them, dragging their weapons from their holsters and tossing them in a heap in the center of the room.

"All right, Zanders, and you, Jim Croll, and Mullaby—" Cliff ordered, when the last weapon had been removed from its holster.

"Plum will escort the three of you across the street to the jail. You're all under arrest for disturbing the peace, for attempted arson, and possibly murder."

He turned and nodded to Roney. "Keep the rest of them here under your scatter-gun until we come back, Tim."

"Sure and I will, with pleasure," the Irishman snorted. "And the first man to make a break'll get a bellyful of buckshot."

There were plenty of threats from the three men as they were marched across the street and into the jail. And they were not idle ones, either. Their temper was at fever pitch. If any one of them had had a gun, he would have turned and tried for the medico's scalp, even at the risk of his own life. But they knew Dorr Plum and they knew the physician. Both of them could shoot fast and straight, as had been demonstrated many times in the past. Doctor Cliff Monroe might be a physician, but no man in the county could outdraw him, and they knew it.

Plum locked the three of them in separate cells, called Shorty Weaver from the stable, and ordered him to stand guard. With the cries and the curses of the prisoners ringing in their ears, Cliff and Dorr marched determinedly back to the Lone Deuce. The punchers, herders and hired gunnies were in the same position as when they had left. Not one of them had had the temerity to attempt a break under the threatening muzzle of Roney's scatter-gun.

Plum and the physician took them outside two at a time, and watched them mount their ponies and go hightailing it out of town towards their homes spreads.

"What do you figger to do now?" the old sheriff asked, when the last man had shaken the dust of Painted Springs from his boots.

"I'm counting on the settlers' wives to hold their men in line," the medico replied. "But there's one missing, and you and I have got to find him tonight. We can't afford to leave Jeffries out of this."

"Wait until I say hello to Maw," Plum suggested. "She's most likely worried about me and where I been."

"That's a good idea," the medico answered with a grin. "Maw can be a lot of help to us, if she wants to. I think I've figured out the right solution. It isn't the men who suffer at times like this; it's the women. We've already lined up the settlers' wives. Now if we could get Mrs. Croll and the ranchers' wives to side with us, it would be a simple matter to iron things out."

Roney had replaced his shotgun behind the counter, and he listened attentively as the physician talked. "I'll help," he announced. "There ain't no use of me stayin' open the rest of the night. Although I ain't overly friendly with the sheepmen's wives, maybe I could get 'em to see what's what."

"Thanks, Tim, but perhaps you would be of more service watching the jail. As long as Jeffries is loose, there is always the possibility of his trying to release the prisoners."

Whereupon Cliff and Plum marched across the street to the Mansion House. Maw Blane, after the medico had told her what he and Plum were trying to do, agreed to help all she could.

"I'll call on Mrs. Croll in the morning, Cliff," she said. "You're right about the women. They can stop it better than anyone can, for they are the ones who suffer. I'll tell them you want them in town tomorrow night. And you can use my dining room for the meeting."

"That's fine, Maw. I knew we could count on you."

Her glance rested on the old lawman. "Dorr," she snapped, "you're too old a man to go gallivanting around the range at this time of night. You let the doc handle this. I declare to goodness, you look as though you hadn't slept in a week."

"Don't you start ridin' herd on me yet," the old lawman grumbled testily. "Bonnett's gone, and there ain't no one else for Cliff to depend on. Come on, Son. We've get a heap of ridin' to do tonight. There's Jeffries to be found and locked up."

The two men turned out again into the night. They marched to the jail first to see if their prisoners were all right. Jim Croll, locked behind the steel bars of a cell for the first time in his life, was not too friendly, but he had cooled off some, and was beginning to realize that perhaps a night in the jail would at least give him a good night's rest. Mullaby, a fatalist at heart, and worn out besides was already sound asleep on his iron cot.

But not the fire-eating Zanders. The man could swear like a mule-skinner, and he called Plum and the physician every name he could think of.

"Right good cussin' for a man who attends church every Sunday," the old sheriff remarked, as the two again turned out to the street, leaving Roney and the hostler to guard the prisoners. "I'd never have thought it of that jigger. And if I told his wife, I'll bet she wouldn't believe me."

They reached their ponies and lifted themselves to the saddle. Plum grunted, "This night ridin' and livin' in a durned cave ain't helped my rheumatiz none. I'll be glad when it's over." And then he suddenly exclaimed, "Gawd Awmighty! I clean forgot about my critters. Maybe they're starvin' to death."

"You'll have to forget the bunnies for tonight," Cliff snapped. The death of a few rabbits meant nothing to the medico when men's lives were at stake.

Plum glanced at the physician's stubborn jaw and sighed, "I reckon you're right, Cliff. Come on. Let's dust."

Side by side, they struck off across the range towards the S Bar 8. It had seemed strange to both men that the sheep rancher had not been among those men who had gathered in town, and they had no assurance that Jeffries would be home, but they were hoping for the best. At a steady lope they crossed the prairie, until the lights of the sheep ranch twinkled at them in the distance.

"We'd better prowl from here," the physician said, slowing up.

"And maybe get a slug for our pains?" the old lawman ejaculated. "Durned if I will. I'm ridin' right up to the front door. Maybe I ain't got a star to wear no more, but I got a pair of good guns that I borrowed from Jim Croll."

Thus they continued to the ranch house. Sam Husker, the sheepman's foreman, heard the strike of their ponies' hoofs and came out to meet them.

"You can't see the boss," he said, when Plum had told him why they had come. "He's sick."

The physician's glance concentrated on the burly foreman's black-hooded eyes. He sensed instantly that the man was not telling the truth, and he swung from his pony and said, "I'm the physician in this county. If Jeffries is sick, I'd better have a look at him."

Husker immediately barred his way. "The boss left orders that he wasn't to be disturbed," he growled. "He don't want a medico."

Cliff was armed, but he wore a weapon so seldom that he had forgotten the gun at his side. He stepped back, planted his feet firmly, and brought his fist up from his side, driving it for the point of the sheepman's jutting jaw.

Husker's hand had dipped for his gun and locked to the butt, but the medico's fist snapped his head back. He went sprawling backward as if a mule had kicked him and lay flat on the ground. Cliff, darting forward, wrenched the gun from his fingers and hurled it into the brush.

Plum dropped from his horse with a rope in his hand. Before the man could recover from the blow to his jaw, his hands and feet were tightly bound.

"There's something queer about things here," Cliff whispered. "I don't think Jeffries is home. We'd better take a look. The rest of this ranch is mighty quiet for this time of night."

Leaving the foreman there on the ground, the two men softly opened the door and peered inside. A light was burning brightly in the living room, but it was empty, as was the rest of the house. Jeffries' bed had not been slept in, nor was there any heat left in the stove.

The two men went out again. Husker could talk now, and he glared up at them wolfishly, a string of epithets coming from his lips. But the color drained from his face when the medico said, looking down at him, "You'd better talk, Husker, if you want to save your skin. We've got a warrant for Jeffries' arrest. He's wanted for the murder of Jan Jungward." It was a chance shot in the dark. Cliff had always suspected that the sheep rancher knew more about that killing than anyone else, but he did not have a shred of proof. He was just bluffing.

The sheep foreman rose to the bait like a hungry bass to a worm. "I didn't have nothin' to do with that," he croaked, fear widening his dark eyes. Honest to God, Sheriff! I wasn't with the boys when they rode that night."

Plum gave a surprised gasp and looked at the medico. "Maybe we'd better get this straight, Cliff," he remarked. Then his glance swiveled down to concentrate on the foreman's face. "Are you willin' to turn state's evidence to save your own skin?"

Fear had definitely gripped the burly foreman now, and was having its way with him. He knew sheep, but he had never been a hired gunhand, nor had he approved of some of his employer's methods. Loyalty to his boss alone had kept him in line. That, and the good wages that Jeffries paid him.

"I'll talk," he whined. "I'll talk if you'll let me go free."

Taking no chances, the two men lifted him and carried him inside the house, where they stretched him out on the sofa. Cliff found pen and ink and a blank tally book on the sheep owner's desk.

"All right," he said. "Talk slowly. I'm going to take down what you say, and you're going to sign it. If you tell the truth, you can fork your horse tonight and hightail it."

Husker did not need any prodding. He told a straight story. Clem Jeffries was the man in back of the movement of settlers into Brant County. He had planned things carefully for a long time. He wanted the nestors to get the cattlemen stirred up. He had helped nearly every family that had come into the county to get started. Henry Rogers had worked hand in glove with him. Jeffries, through the storekeeper, had extended credit to the nestors, getting them all deep into debt.

Jan Jungward had been the only one who had refused to follow the sheepman's advice. Jeffries and his men, in retaliation, had burned Jungward's spread and, when the man had fought back, had killed him. Mrs. Jungward and the boy had been taken out of the country and sent back whence they had come. Jeffries would have done the same to Shan, except for the fact that she had been under the medico's roof. And since she had disappeared, the sheepman had been hunting her day and night.

Only the night before Jeffries' gunnies had cut the trail of the settler raiders. The sheep owner now was out with his men. They intended to take the girl alive, if they could, and bring her back here to the S Bar 8. Jeffries wanted to marry her. Shan Jungward knew too much. He was going to close her mouth by one means or another.

Finished at last, the foreman looked at the clock that ticked away over the stone fireplace. "They've been gone now since before supper," he cried. "If you're aimin' to save my skin as you promised, you'd better let me loose. I ain't hankerin' to face Clem Jeffries after what I just told you."

"Untie him, Dorr," Cliff said grimly, "I think we've got enough evidence now to break Clem Jeffries' back." And when the foreman was loose, he added, "Now just put your name to this, Sam; then you can go."

Husker signed his name on the tally book and turned for the door. The strike of hoofs coming from the prairie stopped him, and his face twisted with rage and fear. "It's too late," he whined. "That's Jeffries and the gunnies comin' back now. Damn you!" He whirled and made a sudden dive for the old lawman.

# CHAPTER SEVENTEEN

PLUM didn't have time to get out of the way. Husker's attack was savage, and he was a big man. His body struck the old lawman, and his arms locked about the ex-sheriff's legs. Plum was bowled over backwards like a ninepin.

Cliff rammed the tally book into his pocket and leaped for his friend. He dragged his gun from its holster and, gripping it by the muzzle, clubbed the big foreman over the head, knocking him completely cold with the second blow.

"The sheep-stinkin' polecat!" Plum gritted, as he rolled himself out from under the unconscious man. "I might have known he wasn't to be trusted." And then he suddenly remembered that their horses were ground-hitched in front of the house. "Gawd Awmighty, Cliff!" he exclaimed. "We're trapped here. Jeffries'll see them ponies, and smell a rat pronto."

The medico made swift tracks for the front door and peered out into the night. He could not see the riders yet, but the beat of the hoofs was louder, and they were evidently coming not from the direction of town, but from the west, where the desert lay. There was no possible way to get the ponies out of sight, nor could he frighten them off. The beat of their hoofs would warn the sheepman and his gunnies.

There was only one answer to his problem. He ran out, grasped the reins of the two ponies, and pulled them toward the house, leading them up the stairs, across the veranda and into the living room.

"Have you clean lost your mind?" the old lawman demanded.

"Not quite," Cliff answered with a sly grin. "I couldn't figure any other place to hide them except inside. Starweather's old bedroom is down the hall. We'll put the ponies in there. I know this house like a book. Drag our friend Husker into Nancy's old room."

Taking them one at a time, Cliff led the ponies down the long hall and into the big bedroom that had once been occupied by the original owner of the ranch. It was customary to fill the homemade mattresses with either hay or straw, and Cliff ripped one from the bed, slit it open with the front sight of his six-gun and spread the hay in front of the ponies. It was old and dry, but the animals seemed to like it. And it might at least keep them quiet.

the doorway, watching him. "Husker's roped and the doorway, watching him. "Husker's roped and tied to the bed," he whispered, "and I gagged the lousy woolly nurse, just to play safe."

"Good! Then let's get out in front where we can listen and learn, Dorr. We'll hide in that room that's next to the parlor."

Noiselessly now, for the two could already hear the creak of saddle leather and the clank of spur and bit chains, they crept down that long hall and into the bedroom where Nancy's guest, Claire Napier, had slept.

The old lawman broke the silence by whispering hoarsely, "I can hear 'em comin'."

Boots were stamping around the corner of the house, and Jeffries' strident voice lifted.

"Dang your hide, Sam! Where in tarnation are you?"

The partition that separated the rooms was made of boards, and there were places where the wood had warped and thin streaks of light showed. The old lawman and the physician glued their eyes to one of these, scarcely daring to breathe for fear their presence would be detected.

The wide-shouldered sheepman stamped across the veranda and into the living room, his flat-heeled shoes sounding like hammers. Cliff, peering through the crack, saw his bulky body framed in the door, and he saw, too, in back of him, the crumpled figure of Shan Jungward being supported by two men. Crimson smeared her lovely face, and her grey flannel shirt was torn almost to ribbons.

The physician ripped out a choked exclamation of dismay. Plum's steely grip on his arm silenced him. "This game ain't over yet, not by a jugful," he whispered. "The dirty son! I never did like Clem Jeffries, and I'd sure like to put a slug through his gizzard right this minute, just to see him squirm."

The bright light of the lamp seemed to bring the girl out of the daze she was in. Cliff saw her wrench herself away from the two gunnies holding her and stalk into the living room.

Jeffries was oily and pleasant. "Sit down, Shan," he said. "I've wanted to have a talk with you for a long time." He then addressed the two gunhawks, who were watching with curious and speculative eyes. "Go find Sam Husker," he barked at them. "Damn his soul! I told him to stay here and watch the house. I'm finished with him. He's too softhearted and squeamish for his job. Get, now."

The two men turned out into the night, and Jeffries seated himself at his desk. Cliff could not see him through his crack in the wall, but the sheriff could, and he whispered, "He's lookin' for somethin' that he can't find, and he acts a mite worried."

Then, suddenly, the sheepman's voice was raised stridently. "I'll wring that foreman's neck," he rapped out. "I'll teach him to go snoopin' around my desk."

Shan did not answer. All of the spirit seemed to have been knocked out of her. Her face was white, and she held her neckerchief against her crimson-smeared cheek.

Boots stamped across the veranda, and Cliff saw the hatted face of one of the gunnies peer through the door. "We can't find hide nor hair of Sam," the man announced. "He ain't in the bunk house, and he don't seem to be here at all."

"I might have known I couldn't trust him," Jeffries blazed. "All right! Forget it. Throw a guard around the house, Jug-Eye. We don't want any unwelcome visitors tonight. I'm not expectin' any trouble with the nestors, but that meddlin' medico is loose again, and so is Plum. Between the two of them, they can stir up a nest of trouble. If anyone comes visitin', you shoot first and ask questions afterwards."

The man left, and Jeffries turned his glance on the girl, studying her, his eyes avid with desire. "Now, girl," he said, with a crooked smile, "we're alone. I'm goin' to lay my cards on the table."

"They're dirty cards," Shan blazed at him, "and you don't need to show 'em. I know 'em by heart. Why did you bring me here?"

"I've had my eye on you for a long time, Shan," the sheepman said softly. "I'm a bachelor, and I ain't married 'cause never, until now, have I seen the woman that I figured was good enough."

"And you think I am?" Shan raised her eyes and looked at him. She took off her dust-encrusted hat and ran her fingers through her bright hair. With the lamplight full on it, it blazed like a bonfire in a high wind.

"Not so fast," Jeffries mocked. "I'm too old a bird to be caught by just a pretty face. I callate you could be made over to suit me. That's what I mean. You're young and you're pretty. And I'm thinkin' that, under that mop of red hair, you've got a good head."

"Other men have told me that. Come to the point, Jeffries."

"All right, I will." He tapped his fingers on the desk nervously.

Cliff and the old lawman had their eyes glued to the cracks, and were straining their ears to catch every word. So absorbed were they that, for the moment, they had both forgotten that the man they wished to arrest and imprison was alone and theirs for the taking.

"This is my proposition, Shan." Jeffries' glance was focused on Shan, and his eyes were like hot rivets. "It'll be only a matter of time 'fore I'll own this range. You've been of great service in stirrin' up the cowmen against the settlers. That's exactly what I planned. I want Jim Croll's spread, I want Zanders'. But I'm aimin' to buy 'em cheap, when they're broke from fightin' the hoemen. Now I can do one of two things with you. If you'll marry me, I'll make you the richest woman in this state."

"And if I don't?" she asked.

"Let's not auger about that, girl," he suggested. "You're young, and you want to live."

"I'm still askin'," she rapped out. "You wouldn't dare kill me as you killed my dad!"

"So you know that." The sheepman's voice was suddenly menacing and venomous. "That's all the more reason why I'd do just that. There's no law here in Brant County. Bonnett's in a safe place, where he can't raise a finger to enforce it. Dorr Plum has no authority, and won't have. I've got too much power to let the county board appoint him over my objections. As for the meddlin' medico, they'll pick him up some day soon on the desert with a bullet through his back."

Cliff saw Shan's eyes blaze and her body straighten as she leveled her glance on the sheepman. "Now I'll talk, Mr. Woolly Nurse," she snapped. "I don't tie my wagon to a horse that's already outlived its usefulness. I don't think you've got a Chinaman's chance of ever ownin' the S 4, the Squared X, or any of the other spreads in this county. And what I did wasn't done on your say-so or to please you. I figured you were the one that killed dad, but I wanted proof. I've got it now, and I'm goin' to live to see you get your sheep-stinkin' neck stretched all out of shape."

A shrill neigh that seemed to come from the center of the big ranch house startled both the girl and Jeffries, and made the old lawman behind the partition curse softly. The sheepman got swiftly to his feet, crossed the room and peered down the long hall.

Shan broke the silence with a derisive laugh. "Do you stable your broncs in the house, too, along with the hogs?" she asked mockingly.

"Damn you!" the sheepman grated, and whirled to face her. "No woman can make fun of me and remember it."

Cliff had seen enough. Anger had gripped the sheepman now; the girl's mocking voice had driven him to a killing mood. Cat-footed, with his gun palmed and leveled, Cliff slipped from the room, snaked the few steps to the living room, and stood there just behind Jeffries' back.

"Lift them, Clem," he commanded, "or you won't live to feel your neck stretched."

The medico saw the neck muscles of his opponent swell and grow taut. He saw the man take a deep breath and then, with a whirling motion, throw his body aside as his hand streaked for his gun. Cliff thumbed the hammer of his weapon, but the slug went wild, making a small star-shaped bloom on the wall.

Shan screamed as she saw Jeffries, with killer lights flecking his eyes, level his weapon at the medico, and she hurled herself across the room, straight for the sheepman. Savagely he tried to fend her off, but the impact of her body knocked him off balance.

The physician did not try for another shot, for Shan's body was in the way, and there was too much risk of hitting her. He dropped his weapon and dove for Jeffries, smashing his fist at the sheepman's exposed face. At the same time the girl got her fingers locked to the muzzle of Jeffries' gun and tried to wrench it loose. Failing in this, she sunk her teeth into his wrist.

Clem, managing to duck Cliff's blow, swung around and struck the physician hard with his shoulder. Then, with a vicious oath, he doubled the fist that had held the gun and drove it hard into the girl's face. Blood spattered his hand as it smashed her lips back against her teeth, and sent her sprawling and whimpering backward.

Hunching his big shoulders and trying to use his head for a battering ram, he drove for the medico's middle like a charging bull. Plum, standing in the doorway with both guns leveled, was trying to find a mark to shoot at. Each time he got the sheepman's body under his sights, the medico's head or shoulders would blot it out.

Now that the big sheepman stood in front of him, trying every device known to cruel fighting, the medico had suddenly become as cold and merciless as he, and he started to work with venomous efficiency to beat this man to a plup. He forgot that there were men outside, hired gunnies, who would naturally come to the sheepman's rescue at the first shot.

The old lawman had not forgotten that, though, and tried to do something about it. He had no chance. A slug came winging out of the darkness in back of him, and the sudden white light that exploded in his brain dropped him into an abyss of darkness from which there was no escape.

Men came crowding in the door, lips bared, guns out and ready for the kill. But they did not try to shoot the medico. Every brush popper loves a fight, and here was one that was worth watching.

Jeffries tripped Cliff, sent him sprawling on his back, and then leaped on top of him, his thumbs gouging for his eyes.

Cliff doubled his legs beneath him, sent the sheepman catapulting across the room, and followed him with a running dive and tackle that knocked over a chair and crumpled its legs.

The sheepman extricated himself by two vicious boots of his heavy shoes to the physician's stomach. Cliff retaliated with a wicked blow to Jeffries' middle, a blow that expelled all the wind from his lungs and doubled him over. The physician's fist followed that with a bone-cracking jar that lifted the burly sheepman clean from his toes, arched his back, and sent him flying over to end up in a sitting position against the wall, his eyes glazed.

"All right, Doc," a gunny barked, grinning widely and leveling his weapon at Cliff. "You've won that round fair and square, but I reckon there ain't goin' to be a second one. Hunker over ag'in' the wall. Get a pail of water, somebody. Clem's needin' a bath after that last haymaker the medico leaned on him."

Wiping the blood from his eyes, Cliff saw Shan sitting on the floor with her back to the sofa. She was holding her neckerchief to her bloody lips, and her eyes were staring unseeingly at the opposite wall. Plum lay as he had fallen, arms outstretched, face down, with Jim Croll's two guns still gripped tightly in his gnarled fists.

Weary almost to the point of exhaustion, Cliff leaned against the wall and tried to control his labored breathing. He and Plum had failed after all. Jeffries was not dead, but the ex-sheriff probably was. And Cliff knew the sheepman for what he was, a killer. Not one of them would come out of this alive. Jeffries could not afford to take that chance.

Two men lifted the sheepman to the sofa, and another poured water over his face and shoulders. That cold douche brought him to; his grey eyes focused on Cliff, then on the inert form of the ex-sheriff, and then on the girl.

He struggled to a sitting position, and his glance clashed with the medico's. "You won the fight, Doc," he said wolfishly, "but I'm winnin' the game. Take the three of 'em out to the barn, Husky. Put a good noose around the neck of each of 'em and string 'em up. Maybe Plum ain't dead—I'm hopin' he'll feel the rope around his gullet."

The gunny called Husky turned to the physician. "Pick up your friend," he ordered. "You ain't too weak."

Cliff did not argue the matter, for he could see no out for any of them at that moment. He rolled his friend over and lifted him up, swinging him across his shoulder so that Plum's head hung down, and strode to the door.

"Look at that danged lawman," one of the men exclaimed. "His hands is still grippin' his guns."

Cliff had noticed that, too, and had wondered about it, until the ex-sheriff's heart had pressed against his shoulder. Then he knew. For Dorr Plum was far from dead. He was playing possum until the odds were right. But he was giving a perfect imitation of a dead man, and when one of the men tried to pry a gun loose from his clutching fingers, the medico gritted:

"Rigor mortis has set in, you fool. Let him die like a good lawman, with his guns in his hands and his boots on."

In that way, without looking at the bruised and pulpy face of the sheepman, but supremely conscious of the girl who walked behind him under the drawn weapons of Jeffries' gunmen, Cliff stalked out into the night, around the house, and headed for the barn.

# CHAPTER EIGHTEEN

DUSKY, the big gunny whom Jeffries had put in charge of the execution, strode directly in back of the medico, whose shoulders drooped under his heavy burden. Plum's head hung down limply across Cliff's back, and his two hands, dangling loosely, but still gripping the guns, thumped the back of the physician's legs with each stride.

The girl seemed to be punch drunk from the wicked blow Jeffries had smashed into her face. Cliff would have helped her if he could, but it took all his strength to carry the body of the old lawman. Dorr Plum wasn't fat, but there was plenty of beef on his old bones.

Flanking the prisoners on both sides were two more of Jeffries' hired gun-toters, swaggering gun-hung men whose faces showed no mercy.

With the medico and the ex-sheriff out of the way, with Poke Bonnett a prisoner somewhere, the county would be at the sheepman's mercy.

The physician wondered about the big sheriff as his boots trod a slow pace across that wide yard. The man's disappearance was a complete mystery. Bonnett was a careful, cunning lawman, and a man who would be hard to hold a prisoner, and harder still to capture. Cliff could not imagine any trumped up tale that would suck him into a trap when he was on his way to Yuma with a prisoner. But, according to reports, his prisoner was dead: his corpse had been found with that of one of the other men who had stopped the stage and asked for transportation. Cliff guessed that Bonnett had killed the two of them before the other man had managed in some way to knock him out.

The huge black opening of the barn door now yawned in front of him and, at the command of Husky, he stopped. "Git a lantern, Slim," he ordered, "and three lariats. It looks to me like a waste of time to hang Plum, but them was the boss' orders."

Standing there, listening to the labored breathing of the girl beside him, Cliff murmured, "Keep your chin up, Shan. You're not dead till the rope tightens."

Husky heard that, and a wicked grin creased his thin lips. "The doc's right, gal," he echoed. "And the higher you keep your chin, the sooner your spine'll crack. It's better than dyin' with a slug in your belly."

"How do you know, my friend?" Cliff demanded softly. "Don't tell me you've been hung, and that you're just a ghost."

"I've seen enough of 'em hang," the man retorted derisively, "to know. This ain't the first time I've fitted a noose about a neck. You and the gal don't need to worry none. You're lookin' at an expert. I'll fix the nooses so they won't slip."

A light came flickering across the yard, and the gunny with the lantern and the lariats over his arm stamped up. Once again the procession moved forward, and entered the barn.

Cliff eased the ex-sheriff's heavy body to the dirt floor, a little surprised to find Plum's body as stiff as a poker. He had to lay him on his side, for the old lawman had his muscles tensed and refused to be straightened out. The sheep gunny, noticing that, came over and peered down at him.

"Can't you straighten the old coot out?" he demanded. "He'll look like a jackknife, swingin' in the breeze thataway."

The physician shook his head. "I told you that rigor mortis has set in. In plain English, that means that the joints have locked and the muscles hardened in death. You can hang him if you want to, but Dorr Plum will never know it."

Husky took the lantern from the other man and swung it across the old lawman's face. Plum's eyes were wide open, apparently sightless and staring straight ahead. He did not even blink. And when Husky kicked him savagely in the chest with his heavy boot, not a muscle of Plum's face twitched. It was a tense moment for the physician, for he knew how much will power it took for Plum to keep from crying out. It almost convinced him that his friend was dead.

Husky handed the lantern back to the other man. "Ain't no sense in hangin' a corpse," he growled. "Just fix two of them ropes, Slim. Use that big beam over there. All right, Doc. You and the gal turn around. I'm tyin' your paws behind you, so you can't grip the rope."

Once they were tied, he moved off toward the other two men, leaving Cliff and Shan towering over the body of the lawman.

Plum's voice, soft and almost indistinguishable, came up to him then. "I'll wait till they get the light further away, maybe till they get you both on the ponies."

Husky heard words spoken, and his glance narrowed on Cliff and the girl. "Talkin' to yourself?" he growled. "Sayin' your prayers? If you ain't, you'd better."

"I was raised a Christian," the physician replied quickly, "and that's exactly what I'm doing. It wouldn't do you murderers any harm, either. Try a prayer some time—just before they tighten the rope around your neck."

"Bah!" the man grated back.

"Spoken like a real sheepman," Cliff retorted. "But what's the matter? Are your fingers all thumbs? I could have had those ropes fixed an hour ago."

The sheep gunny laughed, and the other two men grinned. "That's the first time I ever heard of a man bein' in a hurry to die," he remarked. "All right. Just come this way, and don't try any funny business. Jeffries said to hang you, but I reckon he wouldn't kick a lot if I just put a slug or two through your hearts."

Shan leaned against the physician for support, too dazed to hear the sheriff's reassuring words. Tomtoms were beating in her head, and she was still dizzy from that cruel blow on her lips. The wound on the side of her head had opened again, and a thin trickle of crimson was oozing down her cheek.

"Courage, Shan," Cliff whispered as they moved across the barn to the two waiting nooses. "Keep your chin up."

He saw her throw her head back, and felt her muscles stiffen. "At least," she whispered softly, "we're goin' out together, Cliff. I'd ought to be thankful for that."

Husky slipped the noose over the physician's head first, and then over Shan's, drawing both loops tight, but not enough to choke them.

"All right, Slim. Bring in the ponies. I reckon we're all set now."

Cliff, standing there with that rough rope around his neck, felt far from comfortable. He had to grit his teeth to keep them from chattering. If Plum did not open up pretty soon on these three men, he was afraid it was going to be too late.

Then, suddenly, Slim reappeared in the door with two horses and led them inside the barn. For a moment the three men were grouped together, with the prisoners in front of them and the ponies in back of them.

It was the opportunity for which the old lawman had been waiting. His strident voice came out of the shadows like the beat of swiftly traveling hoofs.

"Freeze, you mutton-eaters! I've got a gun in each fist, and I'll gut-shoot the whole three of you if you so much as bat an eyelid."

The eyes of the three men widened in shocked and benumbed surprise. Two of them began slowly to raise their hands. Husky, the toughest of the lot, did not seem to have even the power to do that. All the color had drained from his face, and his lower lip was trembling as if with the ague. With a choked scream of fear, he suddenly whirled and made a running dive for the safety of the outside.

The ex-sheriff's gun blazed once, the staccato boom of the gun reverberating from the barn walls. Husky staggered, tried to save himself, but couldn't. With a choked scream that was more animal than human, he pitched forward on his face, right beneath the hoofs of the two horses. Both of them reared instantly, and Cliff saw the steel-shod hoofs of one of them drop down to crunch the gunny's life blood out.

"You two'll get the same," Plum cried menacingly to the other men, as he snaked forward out of the darkness into the slanting rays of the lantern light. He shoved one gun back into its holster, brought his pocket knife from his pocket, opened it with his teeth, and slashed the ropes that bound the medico's wrists. "You cut the gal's, Cliff," he ordered. "I ain't takin' any chances with these two hombres."

A voice hailed them from the house. "What's the trouble out there?"

Plum, taking the guns from the two sheepmen, prodded one of them in the back, and whispered, "If you don't want your innards spread all over the barn, answer that jigger. Tell him it was just the medico tryin' to make a break, and that you had to crease him."

The man's voice lifted instantly, repeating almost word for word the old lawman's instructions. It seemed to satisfy the sheepman up at the house, for he called back, "Jeffries says to hurry up and string them jiggers up. There's still a lot of work to be did tonight."

The man did not answer, and for a good reason. Plum had brought the butt of his gun down on the sheepman's head, knocking him completely cold. Cliff had cut the girl's bonds, but he had to put his arm around her to keep her from falling, and her own fingers did not even have strength enough to lift the noose from her neck.

"We got to get out of here pronto," Plum gritted. "But I'm aimin' to give that sheepman a taste of his own medicine." He forced the man who was still standing to move beneath the noose.

"You goin' to hang me?" the fellow whimpered.

"Sure! But not by the neck. Shan! Quit bein' a baby, and let loose of the doc. Cliff! Tie this gent's hands behind him and his feet together, and stuff his neckerchief in his mouth. I'm goin' to hoist him up and let him do a little trapeze performin' for a spell."

Cliff liked the idea. It would not hurt either of the men, but it would give them a chance to think over their sins, while they were dangling from the end of a rope. Both of the gunnies were bound and gagged and lifted into the air, where they hung from the rafters, at first kicking and squirming, then finally quieting down, their glances leveling evilly on the two men who stood below and grinned up at them.

Plum blew out the lantern.

Cliff said, "You'd better let me tie something around that head of yours, Dorr. You've got a nasty crease in your scalp."

"To heck with that," the old lawman barked testily. "My head's all right. It ain't the first time I've had it creased by a slug. How are we goin' to work this now? Seems like I remember Jeffries tellin' his men to throw a guard around the house. If we try a break, we're liable to get gunned down pronto. Our broncs are still in the house, and I don't trust these S Bar 8 cayuses."

Their dilemma was resolved for them. A man's voice lifted furiously from the yard. "Clem," he yelled, "them jiggers didn't hang, after all. They gunned Husky down, and they got Slim and Honey tied and prisoners in the barn."

Men's boots beat on the sun-baked ground, and the three hidden in the barn could hear the thud of hoofs encircling their prison, surrounding them. Jeffries came barging out from the house, his body silhouetted for a split instant by the light in back of him.

He gave swift orders. Gunfire laced the night in a sudden volley, and lead came pouring into the barn like a swarm of angry hornets. Cliff knocked Shan to the floor. One of the horses reared as a slug creased him. With shrill neighs of fear, the ponies plunged ahead, straight through the barn, and with a rending crash struck the opposite door, knocked it from its hinges and vanished into the night.

Plum rasped hoarsely, "There goes our transportation. Daggone it! I thought sure that sheepman was deader 'an a salt mackerel. He must have bellied his way outside while we was stringin' them other two up."

Muffled cries came from the two sheepmen dangling in the air. Bullets were winging by them too close for comfort, and they were jerking and swinging their bodies like a couple of madmen, all to no avail. The more they jerked, the tighter the nooses locked under their armpits.

"A stray slug is liable to end their lives," Cliff said. "Maybe we ought to cut them down."

"Let 'em dangle there," the old lawman rapped out bitterly. "And just let them polecats try to take us prisoners again. We've got five good guns, and four belts filled with cartridges. Shan!"

he rapped at the girl. "I ain't never seen you fold up like this. Take this gun and climb up there into the loft. If we're goin' out, we might just as well go out with our boots on." He pressed a gun and belt into the girl's hands.

"I'll take the back door," Cliff said. "You take the front, Dorr."

The feel of the cold steel in her palm brought Shan out of the daze that had gripped her. She moved swiftly through the darkness and, before Cliff knew it, had her arms around his neck and was pressing her lips to his. Then, suddenly, she laughed and broke away as his body stiffened. Cliff heard her say, as she climbed the ladder that led to the loft, "*Vaya con Dios,* Cliff." Only a few seconds later, he heard her gun chatter a swift death song and a man's smothered scream as a slug caught him.

Cliff had no time to hear much else after that. He could see the stealthy, shadowy forms of Jeffries' gunnies trying to prowl the rear of the barn, and in a moment one of the guns he held was hot, and there was at least one man out there who wouldn't ever again see the light of day.

At intervals he could hear the old lawman's weapon bark, followed by his curse as the shot missed or his exclamation of satisfaction as a slug found its mark. As Cliff reloaded his gun, he listened for Shan's weapon. It was still hammering away up in the loft, and he knew that as yet the girl was untouched by lead.

The firing died suddenly, but not for long. A minute or two later lead was again pouring through the darkness, and Jeffries' raucous voice could be heard yelling commands to his men.

Cliff's fingers ran over the almost empty cartridge belt in his hand. There weren't many left, so he conserved his fire. Shan was apparently doing the same thing.

Someone outside yelled, "Why don't we fire the barn, Clem? Let's burn the jiggers out."

"Hell, no," the sheepman called back. "I just built it—that barn's got all my winter hay left in it—and I ain't honin' to build another one. Come daylight, we'll smoke 'em out."

Once again the thunder of the guns died, and this time they remained silent. Plum crept back through the blackness to whisper to the physician.

"Do you reckon the gal's all right?" he worried. "I ain't heard her move up there."

"I'll go up and see." Cliff left the ex-sheriff, felt his way through the blackness to the ladder and went up hand over hand. It was even darker up there, and he called softly, "Shan!"

A faint moan made him grit his teeth and snake towards the sound. His groping hands touched her face, and he slipped his arm beneath her shoulders. He dared not strike a match to see where she was hit, but, as his hand pressed under her back, something wet and sticky stuck to his fingers, and the girl whimpered.

Her face was just a white blur in the darkness at first, but gradually the oval outline of it became clear and he could see her eyes, deep pools of darkness, staring up at him. He put his head down to listen to her heart beat and found it weak and fluttering.

She tried to move, and then her voice came softly, "I'm goin'—out, Cliff. Hold me tight. I'm scared."

"Damned if you are, Shan," he gritted. He tried to turn her over, but she resisted him.

Her voice came again, and he knew that she was smiling. "Good-bye, Cliff. *Vaya con Dios!*" Her body stiffened suddenly in his arms, and then went limp.

"Damn that Clem Jeffries," Cliff cursed. "I'll kill him if it's the last thing I do!"

# CHAPTER NINETEEN

SHAN JUNGWARD was dead. For a long time Cliff sat there in the darkness of the loft, holding her body in his arms.

The continuous silence from the loft worried the old lawman, hunkered in the stygian blackness below, and he called softly, "Cliff! Cliff!"

The medico picked the girl's body up in his arms and stumbled through the darkness to the ladder. It was a difficult feat to perform, that descent down the narrow rungs, but somehow he made it. He laid Shan on the floor, and found an old horse blanket with which he covered her.

"Shan's dead, Dorr," he whispered bitterly.

The old lawman answered with a volley of vituperation that would have put a good mule-skinner to shame, and then he put his hand on the physician's arm and gripped it hard. "It was a heap better 'an bein' hung or spendin' ten years in the pen. She turned herself into an outlaw, Cliff. If we had won free, we'd still have had to bring her to trial. She'd have had to answer to the law for all them things the hoemen did."

Dorr Plum had always been that kind of a lawman. No matter how good the friend, once he or she went outside the pale of the law, the man or woman was a criminal to be hunted down and, if possible, brought to trial to answer for his crimes. Cliff Monroe had lived by those tenets, too. With Bonnett missing, it would have been his duty to arrest Shan Jungward, lodge her in the jail, and see that justice had its way.

It softened the blow a little to know that he would never have to do that now. Hunkered in the dark, the two men were silent as each became absorbed in his own bitter thoughts.

The gunfire had ceased, and there was no sound from outside, not even the beat of a pony's hoofs. "Maybe layin' a trap for us," Plum whispered.

And then, suddenly, a gun laid a spanging sheet of sound across the night, followed by yells and curses. There was a commotion on the veranda which the two men in the barn could not see. Another gun barked, and another, and then a pony's hoofs beat away, the sound finally dying out.

Jeffries' voice reached the two men hunkered in the barn, but his words were unintelligible. They knew only that he was furious, and that he was cursing someone in no uncertain terms.

"What in tarnation do you suppose happened?" the old lawman ejaculated. "Sounds like some hombre got fed up with the deal and hightailed it."

"I don't know, Dorr, but every time I hear Jeffries' voice, I wish I could get my fingers on his neck. It's too bad I didn't kill him when I had the chance. If I'd shot him in the back when I had him under my gun, Shan would be alive now, and this business would be ended."

"A man can't even shoot a polecat in the back," Plum growled. "It weren't your fault. Lord knows, you tried hard enough to do your duty as the only lawman left in the county. Don't blame yourself for the gal's death. It was fate. I reckon the good Lord had it figured thataway."

Cliff did not answer. His own thoughts were too bitter. It seemed as if fate had singled him out to heap misfortune on his shoulders. Gloom had dropped over him like a blanket, and he could see no way out for either of them. They were surrounded by sheepmen, and Jeffries dared not let them live.

The hours ticked away. A cold draught of air swept through the open barn doors, chilling them both to the bone. But they dared not relax for an instant. Each in turn would prowl to one or the other of the big opened doors and peer out into the blackness. The sky was overcast with ominous clouds, and the smell of rain was in the rising breeze that swept down from the rugged peaks of the Dos Cabezos. Plum complained continually of his stiffening joints. And then suddenly a long, jagged fork of lightning flamed across the heavens, followed by an ear-splitting peal of thunder. Rain began to patter on the shake roof of the barn, swelling into a crescendo of sound as the heavens opened in earnest.

"This is a heap better than bein' out there on your belly, waitin' to shoot a lawman and a medico," Plum remarked with a sour laugh. "Let's snake over close to the doors. With that lightnin', we'll get a chance to see where the jiggers is hidin'. Come daylight, we won't have much chance. I'd like to take as many as we can to Kingdom Come 'fore they make a lead mine out of my carcass."

For a time the two men again took up their hidden positions, guns palmed, eyes straining to pierce the darkness. But the lightning refused to become their ally. No more jagged forks blazed across the heavens; the night was again like a solid wall, thick enough to cut, but impenetrable.

Rain cascaded from the roof, coming down in a steady stream to form huge puddles across the yard, and these widened and grew in extent until the water was running into the barn itself, following the ditches that had been carved out of the dirt in front of the stalls.

"Danged if I'm goin' to stay in this rat hole any longer," Plum growled finally. "We'll only get killed in the mornin', anyhow.

There won't be none of them jiggers out in this—you can bet your last dollar on that. Let's make a break for it."

"All right, Dorr," Cliff replied in a tired voice. "My boots are sopping wet now, and if I stay here much longer I'll have pneumonia."

And then a sound reached his ears that froze the blood in his veins. He gripped the ex-sheriff's arm tensely.

The old lawman's eyes swiveled slowly toward the blanket-shrouded body of the girl; then, with a sudden cry, he leaped across and pulled the covering from her face. It was too dark to see clearly, but he thought he could hear the faint breathing of the girl. Cliff followed him and dropped to his knees beside Shan, taking her wrist in his fingers.

"She's alive, Dorr," he gritted. "God in Heaven! What will we do now?"

The unexpectedness of it had unnerved him. He looked up at the old lawman, trusting Plum to guide him, as he had on so many former occasions.

"Do?" Plum ejaculated softly. "I reckon there's only one thing to do, Cliff. There's a box stall over there. I'll pitch some hay down on it. You can spread the blanket on it and lay the gal there. I'll find that lantern. You've got to save her life if you can."

"For Jeffries to finish?"

"Maybe not for Jeffries," the old lawman answered quickly. "Don't set there a-gawpin' at me. Maybe there ain't no time to lose. She's alive, and if there's a chance to save her, I reckon there ain't no other man in the county except you that can do it."

"But the light, Dorr—" Cliff argued. "Jeffries will see it. If he doesn't kill us on sight, he'll finish us off in the morning."

"I got a feelin' he won't," Plum rapped back. "Don't ask me what it is, but I always did believe in hunches, and I've got one now. Come mornin', I've got a feelin' that our friend the sheepman is goin' to find himself at the end of the trail."

Plum turned and padded off through the puddles of water. Cliff, kneeling by the girl, heard hay tumbling down to the stall. A moment later he heard the lawman's boots scraping down the ladder, and then a match flared in the darkness, a match that was carefully cupped against the cold breeze that swept through the barn.

Cliff picked Shan up in his arms and, with his boots making a sucking noise in the fresh mud, carried her across to the stall. The sudden flare of lantern light threw grotesque shadows on the walls.

Placing the girl gently on the old blanket that Plum had found, he began carefully to rip from her shoulders the tattered remnants of her flannel shirt. Plum had found another blanket, and he held this up in back of the lantern, trying to shield its rays from the men in the house. The lawman's glance kept continually probing the darkness, his ears straining for any sound that might announce one of the sheep gunnies.

Cliff was the surgeon now, all his attention on the work in hand. He had no kit, no scalpel or probe. He had no tools but his two hands and the jackknife that Plum had opened for him. The only water that was available came from the trough in the stall, and he had no way of boiling that. It was one of the chances he had to take. The only thing he could count on was the girl's vitality and good blood to combat any infection that might develop from the unsterile operation.

With gentle fingers he washed loose the bits of undergarment that had dried to the girl's skin. He found that the slug had entered just below the right breast and, lifting Shan carefully, he turned her on her side to examine the back.

"I think the slug went through, Dorr," he gritted, "but I've got to make sure."

Taking the long blade of the pocket knife, he first held it in the flame of the lantern until smoke had blackened the blade, then he swiftly probed the wound. Shan groaned and whimpered as the knife turned, and perspiration beaded the medico's white forehead.

Plum stood like a stone image, his glance riveted to the girl. He seemed to be almost afraid to breathe. He wanted to drag his eyes away from that ghastly figure beneath him, but he could not do it. His old hands trembled as he held the blanket in back of the lantern.

Then suddenly the physician gave an exclamation of satisfaction and laid the crimson-stained knife down on the dirt floor. Blood was oozing from the wound with each beat of the girl's heart. Without looking at the old lawman, Cliff said:

"Get me a handful of mud, Dorr!"

Plum was glad to obey. He dropped the blanket and moved out of the stall, scooped up a gob of the mud and came back. Cliff took it and plastered it back and front over the wound. That done, he stood up, and peeled off his coat, his vest and then his shirt. In a moment he was nude to the waist. The cotton undershirt he tore into strips, bandaged the wound, and then held the strips in place with his own flannel shirt, which he wound tightly around the girl's breast and shoulders. Lifting her to a sitting position, he drew his vest tight over that, and then finished it all by draping his coat around her shoulders and buttonning it.

"You can douse that light now, Dorr," he said.

"Better not," a sharp voice snapped at them from outside the stall, and both men's glances swiveled that way, as Dorr brought up the gun in his hand.

Not until that moment did either of them realize that the rain had ceased, and that already a dirty grey was lighting the east. Four of Jeffries' gunhawks were grouped around the box stall, with their guns trained on the two men.

The sheep gunny who had spoken laughed harshly. "That was a swell operation, Doc, but it's like jumpin' from the fryin' pan into the fire. Still, I got good news for you. Clem's decided that hangin's too good for you." He laughed again, and winked at the other merciless-faced gun-toters. "Drop that cutter, Sheriff, and stand up, or I might take a notion to finish once and for all the good job the doc's just done."

With a dispirited droop of his shoulders the old lawman let the weapon thud to the ground. "Danged sheep-stinkin' jiggers," he muttered. "I just can't seem to get the smell of 'em out of my nose."

"All right, Doc," the gunny ordered. "Pick the gal up and head for the house."

Somebody had already informed Jeffries of the recapture of the prisoners, and he was waiting for them on the veranda as they filed up. His face was creased into a triumphant grin, and it took all the medico's will power to keep from dropping the girl in his arms and flying at him.

"Put her right there on the sofa," Jeffries ordered, "and you two stand over here against the wall. Calico! You and Lefty keep your guns trained on 'em. These two jiggers are plenty tough, as has been demonstrated tonight, so keep your eyes peeled. This time I'm honin' to see 'em get what I planned for 'em."

Plum said, "There's a couple of your mutton-eaters hangin' from the beam out there in the barn, Clem. You might cut 'em down while they're still alive," And when Jeffries' hands clenched and his eyes blazed at the news, he added, "Oh, they ain't hurt none, 'less one of your gunnies' slugs happened to hit 'em."

Jeffries gave swift orders. Two men from the porch could be heard slopping across the muddy yard toward the barn.

For several minutes the sheepman did not say anything more. His evil glance swung from the still unconscious girl on the sofa back to the two men. He seemed undecided about something, until suddenly he looked out of the window and realized that a new day had almost arrived.

"Saddle a couple of broncs for these two jiggers," he ordered one of the men, who lounged in the doorway with a piece of hay in his teeth. "I'm leavin' the gal here. I'll tend to her later."

"How about their own broncs?" the man asked. "They're both in the corral. We're shy of cayuses, what with Sam hightailin' with mine, and the ones that kited when the ruckus started."

Jeffries nodded assent, and then froze motionless, his glance narrowing on the grey horizon which showed through the open door. Fear seemed to grip him and, with an oath, he flung himself outside, shoving the man who stood in the doorway ruthlessly aside.

Now Cliff and the old lawman could hear the steady tramp of feet, the strike of hoofs, and the faint, but unmistakable creak of wagon wheels. Jeffries came back into the room, his face twisted with anger and fear.

Curiosity gripped the two gunnies who had been tallied to guard the prisoners, and they tried to sneak glances at the outside, but their position did not allow them to see anything. And then suddenly the man who had been lounging in the door and whom Jeffries had shoved aside gave an exclamation of surprise and dismay.

"Cripes," he yelled. "The whole of Brant County's marchin' here, and they're all women. Look, Clem. By God! I ain't never seen anythin' like that before."

# CHAPTER TWENTY

IT TOOK a long moment for the meaning of that to sink into the thick heads of the two men guarding their prisoners. They looked at each other questioningly, and then one of them grated, "Sam Husker did that. The dirty son's double-crossed us. He must 'ave." Their glances narrowed on the sheepman, who seemed rooted to his chair, trying to puzzle things out.

For a moment, Cliff and the old lawman were forgotten in this new and unexpected threat, and Plum whispered to the physician, "You take the big hombre. I'll get the other one."

The physician's hand shot out, and his fingers gripped the ex-sheriff's arm hard. "Wait," he said. "Look at Jeffries. He's scared green."

Plum's glance narrowed on the sheepman. It was true. Jeffries' face was drained of all color, and his hands were gripping the edge of the desk, straining so that the knuckles were white. His mouth sagged wide open, and his eyes were almost popping out of his head.

Cliff did not know the real meaning of the tramping boots, the steady strike of hoofs and the rumble of wagon wheels, but, piecing things together, he concluded that Sam Husker, the man they had bound and gagged inside the house, had in some way escaped. That accounted for the shots they had heard and Jeffries' curses. The sheep foreman, anxious to save his own skin, must have ridden straight to town and, finding that the only men who could help him were behind the bars, have appealed to the owner of the Mansion House for help.

Jeffries' glance finally swiveled to the medico's face, and he tried to pull himself together. "What are all them women comin' here for?" he demanded hoarsely.

"That, my friend," the physician replied tersely, "is outraged womanhood on the warpath. It means that the wives of these ranchers and settlers of the county are sick and tired of bloodshed, of having their homes burned. I've no doubt but what they're coming to pay you a visit. You'd better say your prayers, Jeffries. It looks to me like you've reached the end of the trail."

The sheepman sprang to his feet with an oath. "I ain't scared of no women," he rasped out. "Calico! Lefty! Call the men. If them females is lookin' for trouble, we'll give it to 'em. No skirts is goin' to ride herd on me."

The noise of the slowly approaching procession had reached the ears of the other gunnies in the yard, who now came hurrying up to demand an explanation.

The man called Calico, a tall, bitter-faced gunny, turned and faced his employer. "I ain't fightin' no women," he gritted.

"Nor me," the man next to him agreed. "Let's get our time."

Calico's hand dropped to the butt of his gun. "Open the safe, Jeffries, and fork over the *dinero,*" he ordered. "Me and the rest of the boys is pullin' freight—now. We didn't bargain to fight women, and we ain't goin' to."

"Rats!" the old sheepman exploded, his hand streaking for his holster.

But he didn't get a chance to clear the weapon. Calico's gun flamed once, the shot setting up ear-splitting vibrations of sound in the big living room. Jeffries screamed a curse. His weapon thudded to the floor, and he fell back against the desk's edge, gripping his smashed shoulder with his left hand.

"You'll get no pay," he grated furiously.

"I reckon we will," Calico answered stubbornly, leveling his gun at the physician. "Move over to that safe, Doc," he ordered. "That's where Clem keeps his *dinero.* I seen him put it there only yesterday. Reach in and clean it out."

There were muttered grunts of assent from the rest of the gunhawks, who had crowded in behind Calico at the sound of the shot. Cliff shrugged, stepped across the room to the safe and threw open the door. He reached in, pulled all the packages of bills out and, turning, tossed them to the gunhawk.

Jeffries' face was twisted with rage, and he cursed the men whom he had employed. But they just laughed at him, as Calico, taking the bills, counted them swiftly, divided them, and passed them around.

With a wide grin, Calico holstered his weapon, then, and his glance swiveled to the physician's. "From here on, Doc," he said, "it's your deal. You can do what you want with this woolly nurse. Me and the rest of the boys don't want no part of him."

With mocking laughs, the men turned on their heels and hurried outside. Plum found a length of rope, and he and the physician bound the wounded sheepman securely to his desk chair. Before they had finished, they heard the swift drum of receding hoofs, and knew that Calico and the rest of Jeffries' paid gunnies were hightailing it to a safer place.

The two men moved to the door, their glances concentrating on the procession, which was now in plain sight. It brought a wide grin to the faces of both men. Maw Blane, riding a sway-backed old plug that she had commandeered from the livery, was in the lead, alongside bitter-faced Mrs. Suter on a big draft horse. In back of them came Carol Zanders, trying to look prim and neat, but having a difficult time of it, for the women had come through a pouring rain that had drenched them all to the skin.

Mrs. Croll drove a team of paints hitched to a buckboard, and a settler's wife rode the high seat beside her. Stringing out in back of them, as far as the two men could see, came women on foot, on mules and in schooners. They carried no weapons, but they were a grim and fearful-looking lot, from the crowns of their hatted heads to the soles of their muddy boots.

"Doggoned if I ever seen a sight like that before!" Plum exclaimed.

Maw Blane saw the two men on the veranda, and a look of relief crossed her seamed face. She gave a signal with her arm. As if by some prearranged plan, the procession split instantly, part of the women heading toward the rear of the ranch house, and the others moving steadily ahead. Cliff, remembering that he was still nude to the waist, turned and went inside, a little ashamed to meet all these women.

"You damned old fool!" he heard Maw Blane explode at Plum. "It's a good thing I came home."

"Now, Maw," the old lawman answered testily, "ain't no use to fly off the handle. Jeffries is inside, ready for the noose. The rest of his gunnies lit a shuck when they seen you women comin'. And it's a good thing you did get here." Quickly he told the two women what had happened.

"Where's the girl?" Cliff heard Mrs. Suter ask harshly.

"She's inside on the sofa," Plum replied, "and she's mighty bad hurt and in need of attention. Doc didn't have no tools to work with out there in the barn. I reckon maybe you'd better send someone into town for his kit."

"You leave that to me," Maw replied. Reaching into the saddle pocket, she pulled the physician's medicine kit from it, swung down from the old horse and, pushing the old lawman aside, entered the house. Her glance narrowed on Cliff, on the bound and fear-ridden sheepman, and then on the girl. Mrs. Suter came stalking behind her.

"Go get yourself a blanket or somethin', Doc," Maw rapped out, with a twinkle in her old eyes. "You ought to be ashamed, runnin' around like that, lookin' like an Injun."

Swift orders were given by the two women. Shan was picked up tenderly and removed to Nancy Starweather's old bedroom. Jeffries was unceremoniously lifted to his feet and dragged outside. Five husky settlers' wives tossed him into the body of a schooner and stood guard there. Explanations were given as Cliff, working swiftly, removed the bandages from Shan's breast and prepared to give the ugly wound a more thorough cleansing. In just a little while, the aroma of freshly made coffee and frying bacon came wafting into the sick room. The women had taken charge.

Shan opened her eyes finally, as Maw Blane was tucking her in, and smiled up at her. Maw grinned down at her and remarked, "I do declare, Shan Jungward, I think you're even prettier than Nancy Starweather. Now you close your eyes and sleep."

"Are Cliff and the sheriff all right?" Shan asked weakly.

"Certain sure," Maw answered. "Both fit as fiddles, and gettin' their bellies filled with vittles this minute."

It was a full hour later when Cliff and the old lawman, sitting on the veranda and enjoying a well earned smoke, saw a rider top the rise to the north and come thundering towards the ranch house. Both men recognized him and leaped to their feet to yell a welcome. It was Poke Bonnett. Deep lines etched his face, and Cliff could see under the brim of his hat a crimson-stained bandage wrapped across his forehead.

"Is Shan all right?" the big sheriff asked, when the first greetings were over. "Will she pull through, Doc? I just heard the news from one of the nestors' wives I met on the way."

Cliff and Plum exchanged glances, and then the medico smiled and nodded reassuringly. "I think she'll be as fit and pretty as ever in a week or two, Poke. She's sleeping now, but just as soon as she wakes up, I'll let you talk to her. Now tell us what happened to you."

Bonnett sat down on the top step, rolled himself a quirley, and told them. The two men who had stopped the stage had been planted there by Jeffries. Bonnett had guessed that, and had played into their hands on purpose, hoping in that way to find out who had hired the prisoner to kidnap Shan.

"I had 'em figured right," he concluded, "but they caught me off guard. I had to shoot the prisoner, and one of the others, but one of the jiggers conked me over the head with the muzzle of his gun, and the next thing I knew, I was hog-tied and a prisoner in a little cabin in the badlands. It's taken me nigh onto two weeks to fight clear and get here."

He stood up and paced back and forth across the veranda, his face creased with worry. Finally he stopped and looked down at the medico. "Cliff," he said, "I reckon it ain't none of my business, but I just got to know how things stand now. I ain't been able to think of nothin' but that gal. Shan was loco about you when last I seen her. You told me then you wouldn't marry the finest woman on earth. Are you still of the same mind?" Bonnett's long face was red with embarrassment.

Cliff's grey eyes met the frank brown ones of the big sheriff's, and he smiled. "I haven't changed my mind, Poke," he replied. "Shan's a fine girl and, if you lean that way, by all means hop to it. That makes two jobs I'm handing over to you. From now on you're the law in this county, and also the ramrod of Shan's future—if she'll have it that way. Maybe you'd better not wait till she wakes up. Maybe you'd better just go in there now and hold her hand. I know she's been worried about you."

Bonnett did not wait for any more advice, and Cliff turning towards the old lawman, remarked, “I think that just about makes things perfect, Dorr. I’d enjoy a change of clothes and a good bath. Let’s leave the womenfolks in charge and move into town.”

“Gawd Awmighty!” Plum sprang to his feet, wildeyed, “I clean forgot my poor little critters. I’ll bet they’re ’most starved to death.”

“I doubt that,” the medico answered, with a laugh. “By this time, the warrens are probably full to overflowing with young ones. Seems to me I heard you remark once that, if you left them alone, in three years you’d have thirteen million of them.”

THE END

www.ingramcontent.com/pod-product-compliance
Lightning Source LLC
Chambersburg PA
CBHW070932250626
47159CB00009B/3209
* 9 7 8 1 9 5 7 8 6 8 9 7 4 *